ADDICTED

ADDICTED

Just a Taste #2

AYLA COX

Contents

DEDICATION

To all the girls who wasted away with ain't shit men:

May you find a man who eats you like Bruce Bogtrotter ate that cake.

CONTENT WARNING

This book contains adult themes, including elements of BDSM, portrayals of anxiety, domestic violence, physical violence, and recollections of murder and loss.

Please be cautious of your mental health as you enter into this book.

CHAPTER 1
DENISE

Nothing stoked my rage more than a seven-a.m. meeting. This meeting, in particular, was garbage. Being stuck in a frigid conference room when the sun hadn't even risen yet was bad enough, but we were talking about shit that wasn't seven a.m. material.

"It's the fourth quarter."

"Let's end the year strong."

"Now is the time to start planning H1 and mapping out the QP for our newer investments."

Blah, blah, blah. We already knew all this...

Ten of us Principals were seated around one of the bigger conference tables while Xavier, the Chief Operating Partner at Foxx Ventures, talked *at* us. He was trying to build excitement, but, frankly, he was as exciting as soggy cardboard. I really needed him to wrap it up so I could go out and grab some caffeine and get started with my damn day.

This was my first Principal's Quarterly, and it was a huge disappointment.

Part of me wondered if this was why there were rumors that Xavier and Lucian Foxx were on the outs. The man had no passion for the work. He had been here for over a decade, and he still acted like some weirdo banker stuck in 1987.

He could join us in this century by replacing that ill-fitting suit and learning our names instead of referring to everyone as *kid*. Ick.

Xavier droned on and on, and I looked out at the floor. I was expecting a pack of interns, and I was eager to leave. I was also eager for something else.

It had been over two weeks since the party that changed my pussy forever.

I'd done a bad thing.

But I didn't regret it.

I spent an entire night being devoured.

Being seen, touched, caressed, and fucked until I couldn't breathe.

It had been glorious.

And, yes, it was short-sighted.

That didn't stop me from wanting more.

The man was fucking addictive.

My colleague, Hugh—wait, do we call colleagues "colleagues" after they've made us see non-existent colors tied up and spread out like a sacrifice to some long-forgotten god of lust and passion?

Shit... Maybe?

Hugh had turned me inside out, upside down, and every inch of my body felt hot and craved his attention, even now.

The simmer between Hugh and I since that night was—fun. Between the long, knowing looks and the light grazes of his fingertips against mine as we walked by each other, it was something straight out of a Jane Austen novel.

It had me getting to work early and spending the first part of the morning in Hugh's office, just talking, feeling the cord tethering us together growing tighter and tighter. Hell, I even went and got a birth control shot, just in case his dick ended up in my pussy again.

Okay, maybe I was addicted and getting antsy for more than coffee. But, since that was all I could have right now, I needed someone to either inject it into my veins or pour it over my head to cool me the fuck off.

"Alright, kids, get back at it," Xavier said, clapping his hands in a way that he thought was motivating but just punctuated the team's silent annoyance.

We got up and shuffled out back into the office where, thankfully, the heat actually worked. I smoothed my dress as I walked, glad I'd gone for leggings instead of my usual sheer tights this morning.

The olive-green sweater dress popped against my golden-brown skin. With its long sleeves and extra fabric that folded across both sides of my body, it exaggerated my hourglass waist while still clinging to my form. I complimented it with brown-nude leggings and black leather boots. Even with the leggings, I felt compelled to grab the edge of the dress and makes sure it stayed closer to my knees than the edge of my ass cheeks. The curse of titties and ass.

When I turned to walk into my office, Hugh was sitting waiting.

It was like I'd somehow summoned him with sheer force of will. He held up a cup of coffee without turning around. A cup of coffee from my favorite place around the corner. He could warm me up just fine, I knew that. I had to take a deep breath and remember where I was. It was far too early to have such wicked thoughts. Leaving the door open, I bit my lip as I walked towards him.

"Good morning," he said as I walked up to my desk.

He caught my eyes, and his gaze scanned my body, lingering on my mouth. I bit my cheek, feeling heat slink through me. Of the two things I wanted right in front of me, I could only have one. Straddling his thighs was inappropriate with half the office sitting outside my door. The desire must've shown on my face because Hugh cleared his throat and narrowed his eyes.

"Gorgeous, I'm going to need you to take this and sit down before I make you sit down."

That *tone*.

I licked my lips and skimmed my eyes down his navy suit, taking time to look at his thick thighs and the way his shoulder casually hung over the back of the chair before I grabbed the coffee from his hand. The warmth of his skin beneath my fingertips sent a jolt of awareness singing through my body.

Instead of sitting across from him, I leaned against the desk a few inches away from him. He looked up at me and raised an eyebrow while I kept his gaze and took a sip of the coffee. A sinful noise of enjoyment escaped my lips.

Hugh exhaled and brought his own cup to his lips. I watched his other hand tighten into a fist and rest in his lap. He didn't make a sound, and we sat together in charged silence.

I could see the clench in Hugh's jaw. I tightened my thighs together, feeling the heat settling there as desire warmed my blood and knocked off the chill. Turning a bit, I let my leg brush his as I brought the coffee back to my lips and made another delighted sound.

He stood abruptly and I feigned shock.

"Leaving?" I asked.

Our game was getting hotter. From the bulge in his pants, I could tell I was winning. Putting his hand into his pocket, he looked down at me. His face smoothed and became a blank mask.

"Thanks for the morning pick-me-up," I said, my words heavy with amusement.

Hugh tutted. He leaned down towards me, his cheek faintly brushing mine.

"I'm keeping count, naughty girl." His warm breath caressed my ear, and I felt my insides melt at the fiery promise in his words.

Straightening his suit pants, he walked away. I was breathing a little harder and ready to drag him into the nearest room so he could make good on his promise.

God, that man.

There was a lot to like about him. He was funny and could read a room like nobody else, but he also could read me. Really read me. Like, he'd found some book with my life story inside that gave him the key to all my secrets.

I was convinced that he knew when I was on my period because there was always some sweet and salty snack waiting on my desk when my spice level was a ten with anyone but him. But other than knowing a bit about him and his Grams, the man was a vault.

That's why I was so surprised at the party. We were friends and colleagues, but he'd never let me see that fire in his eyes before. It was like he'd let me see a bit of the real him that he kept hidden away. And as much as I wanted to kick the wall down and see all of him, something told me I needed to move slowly.

I had my own shit that I needed to figure out before I even considered taking Hugh up on round two. There was a lot standing between me and the glorious dick, attached to that Adonis of a man.

Just the thought of him made me drip like a faucet. He made me want to spend my days misbehaving. I knew that the sweet torture he'd provide would make me drop to my knees and beg for mercy that I would absolutely never get.

It took me a few seconds to stand up and walk back around my desk. I said a silent thanks that I'd prepped for the interns last night because all I could focus on was the heaviness between my thighs and the hard dick a few doors down that was a solution to my current problem.

Intern orientation took two hours. Two hours of me talking to a group of strangers. I simultaneously loved and hated it. This was my third batch, and it was never not nerve-wracking to be the center of attention in a room with them.

They all tended to have this starving look in their eyes, and they hung on to every word I said. I walked through the welcome presentation and answered all their questions about what the next three months would look like for them and passed out their personalized packets. After a few more questions, they each ran off to shadow their assigned colleagues.

It wasn't until I was in my office that I finally felt like I could breathe.

I was looking down at the city and I couldn't imagine not having this view every day. There was something magical about San Francisco, something a camera couldn't capture. I made the same promise to myself that I always did—I am going to explore more. Not just the places along my commute, but the entire city.

An annoying voice in the back of my head reminded me how eager I was when I first moved into the city and how every weekend, I'd plan something new and fun, and Curtis would convince me to stay home or guilt me for going out and leaving him alone.

Curtis had already changed by the time we moved here.

When I locked eyes across the quad with him at Fresno state nine years ago, he was always quick to smile. He was our Biology 201 TA and he stayed making science-related puns during lab. I thought it was adorable, that he was adorable, so I said fuck it. I walked right up to him and asked for his number. I may have been a tiny bit drunk at the time, but he didn't notice, he just blushed and typed it into my phone.

Six months later, I moved in with him.

He had his own friends that he spent time with. While they went off, a few girls and I would drive into San Jose and San Francisco for our breaks. That's when I fell in love with the city. The architecture, the vibe, the climate... I knew that it was where I wanted to be next.

And, when I finally graduated, I convinced Curtis to come with me. He'd been thinking about going back to live with his family in Nebraska, but it didn't take much to get him to see how big the world was. I wanted us to explore it together.

I'd never entertained moving back to Los Angeles because it felt like a step backward, like doing something for someone else instead of myself.

But Curtis never really settled in here.

Even though he had a master's in biology, he spent his time in sales at sketchy startups, getting fired every few months. He'd never shown any real initiative, and it almost felt like he worked just long enough to be able to collect unemployment checks.

I knew I needed to let him go, I had just held out hope that we'd find our way back to what we had.

We never did.

And, after a few years, I stopped trying.

Once I started working at Foxx it was easier to throw myself into work than worry about us. And when Cleo moved up from Santa Monica, it was easy to fall into a routine that helped me build a life around Curtis instead of with him.

Hell, Curtis hadn't seen me naked in years, which is why I'd been so taken aback when he introduced himself as my fiancé.

Of course, it hadn't taken long for word to spread about my fake ass engagement. The congratulatory bouquet of roses was currently dying on my kitchen table. Curtis read the card and didn't say a word. Neither did I.

I *was* going to explore more. And I was going to start by going home and getting the uncomfortable stuff out of the way and end whatever this was between Curtis and me because it was finally time for me to accept that this wasn't the life I needed to live anymore.

CHAPTER 2
DENISE

I stayed late at work that night.

Of course, I did.

I wanted to put off this conversation as much as I could. But, I had to have it and it had to be today. Avoiding it and staying in this weird limbo was pointless.

The apartment was dark when I walked in, which told me Curtis was well into whatever gaming session he was having in what used to be our spare bedroom. I flicked on the lights and took in our open plan apartment. Even on my income alone, we had a pretty decent place in the city.

It's not like the massive brownstone from Living Single, but it was comfortable enough for small parties and get-togethers, not that Curtis ever wanted anyone to come over.

The second we moved in, I redecorated everything. I knew I wasn't going to be buying a home anytime soon, and I refused to be in a space that didn't look the way that I wanted it to. The walls were a cool gray. I'd painted the accent wall a nice, dark dragon fruit pink.

The couches were off-white and modern, and it went well with the kitchen that had thankfully already been updated.

My favorite space in the living room, the one I spent the most time fixing up, was my reading nook. It rested right against the pink wall with an oversized chair that lived right next to my book collection. It was every book I'd ever owned, neatly and artfully lined up along black metal shelves bolted into the wall.

It was my showstopper. A lot of work had gone into getting everything just right. I'd lined the edges with soft LED lighting that made the room glow, even when the lights were out.

I wondered if taking a few minutes to read and relax would calm my nerves. The door to the spare bedroom was closed. Whenever Curtis had the door closed, he expected not to be bothered. I kicked off my sneakers and threw my briefcase next to the front door.

I could read and cook. Dinner definitely needed to happen before a conversation with Curtis. I was shrugging off my jacket and rattling through quick recipes when I saw it and froze.

There was a box sitting on the kitchen table. A jewelry-sized box. An open, jewelry-sized box that held the gaudiest engagement ring I'd ever set my eyes on.

My body went ice-cold as my stomach pitched back and forth. The taste of acid coated the back of my throat. Everything in me was screaming to run right back out the way that I came in. I breathed deep to calm my stomach which was threatening to throw up all over the counter and walked slowly towards the box.

The horrific ring sat beside a vase of fresh calla lilies.

I couldn't take my eyes off the ring. It was something I would never in a million years pick up to look at, let alone buy to wear every day for the rest of my life.

Before I could process anything, Curtis walked out of the spare bedroom and wandered into the kitchen. He barely looked my way as he grabbed a water bottle from the fridge.

His massive gaming setup peaked out the open door. The second he got laid off, he'd bought all of it. A few weeks later, he sat me down and told me he was sorry, but he couldn't give me his half of the rent because he didn't have it. I should've kicked him out then.

"Good, you're home." Curtis smiled and pointed towards my bedroom. "The washing machine is doing that thing again. Can you take a look at it?"

Okay, maybe it wasn't what I thought it was. Wouldn't this be the moment where he would say something romantic and propose? Asking would allow me to answer and say, *no, you should probably pack your stuff and leave.* Did he think that this was sustainable? That this was a fulfilling life for us both?

He opened the water and frowned, looking at the clock. "Chinese for dinner? It's a little late for you to cook."

I stood stock-still, my mouth agape as he turned and walked towards the room. Had he always been this much of an asshole, or was I just recognizing how bad it had gotten now?

"I'm mid-campaign with one of the boys, I'll eat in here," he said, talking to the wall.

"Oh, I almost forgot," he said, turning to look at me. "I told the jeweler to give me the flashiest he had and set it in platinum. It should fit."

Without a second glance, he turned around and closed the door firmly behind him.

A familiar rage filled me, and I picked up the ring out of the box and immediately noticed that it was way too small. The name of the jeweler was strewn across the lid. I stashed the box in my pocket before throwing my coat and shoes back on before walking out the door.

Rubbing my sweaty hands on my overcoat, I walked out of the building and headed towards the Thai place instead, feeling the light smack of the ring in my coat pocket as I went.

I didn't know what any of that just was, but one thing that made a pit open in my stomach was Curtis spending tens of thousands on a ring that was meant to symbolize a commitment to me, and it was all wrong.

When I was walking home, it all felt so clear. I knew exactly what I was going to say and how I was going to frame it. But now? He hadn't even asked. He'd just left it there for me to find.

This was such a clusterfuck.

I smiled at the hostess and ordered a few things without looking at the menu. Instead of staying inside, I tied my coat tight and stood outside the restaurant where I could think. Pulling the ring out of my pocket, I looked at it, shifting it from side to side and watching it catch the light.

Where did he get the money for this? My fingers ran across the stones, the warmth in my pocket had done nothing to heat them. They were freezing.

I'd thought of this moment since I was a kid.

The perfect ring, the perfect man, the perfect moment.

Everything about this was a nightmare that I had to fix. What had originally started as something I could ignore was now an iceberg that I was going to collide with. Even if I swerved away from it, there was no way it wasn't going to destroy me.

CHAPTER 3
HUGH

When I walked into her office, she was absently organizing her desk. I could tell there was something wrong, but I knew Denny well enough to distract her before I started to ask her questions. She was less on edge if you said something ridiculous to get her out of her thoughts. With the way she was staring off, it was something serious.

Her gaze flitted to her briefcase when she saw me, but she greeted me with a relieved smile.

"Good morning," I said, smiling at her, silently wishing I'd grabbed a coffee for her.

"Hey, good morning." She waved me in. I sauntered over and watched her eyes move up and down my frame as her lips pursed. It was the usual fuck-me pout that she'd somehow only reserved for me. Just that was enough to make my suit pants start to feel tight. Her gaze was lingering, but I didn't tease her for it.

When her eyes fell to my fingers as they grabbed the chair in front of me, my dick hardened at the memory of her, eyes closed and deliciously spread across my desk. Before I could stop myself, I was back there in my office that Friday night...

"Denny."

My words were a warning. A promise.

She was in front of me, her ass up and her pussy full to the brim with our cum. My tongue was on her back, tasting her salty sweat. All I could smell was her. All I could taste was her.

When she'd come all over my fingers earlier, I knew there was no way this woman wasn't going to come all over my face. The deliriousness she had when I teased and denied her, the way her body sang when I spanked her ass and turned it red beneath my palm. This woman was a fucking drug.

With her writhing in front of my dick, it was coming back to life.

I took a breath. This time I was going to fuck her slow, I was going to make her scream and beg underneath me.

"You see what you do to me?" My tongue continued to nibble and suck at her skin, my hands gripping at her sides, feeling the weight of her

stomach beneath my fingers. I bit down a little harder, testing her limits before moving down her back.

I'd always thought she was gentle. That the girl that teased and sparred with me was goo beneath those hot as fuck clothes. But in that bathroom, she showed me that there was more to her, sizzling just beneath the surface. Begging to be teased and fucked, begging to be overcome.

I'd spent so long thinking about this moment, about her. I wanted to be the one to show her everything she was missing.

Feeling my way down to her round ass, I grabbed the skin roughly. She sighed in contentment. That was all it took. I was rock-hard for her, again.

It was clear she was just as addicted to this as I was. The way her body responded to everything I did, demanding more and more.

That pussy deserved this. Denise deserved this.

And if I only had two nights to give her everything I had, I wouldn't waste a second of it.

I kept up the gentle caress of my fingers. I wanted, no, I needed, to hear her keep sighing, to see her glistening and used pussy clench. When I gave her the space to sit up, our cum started to drip down between her thighs.

Her dewy skin winked in the light and the room smelled of us: sweat, sex, my earthy cologne, and a scent that was fruity and uniquely her.

I joined our hands and used our fingertips to continue to caress her skin. She licked her lips, and I fought the urge to lean forward and suck on her tongue.

"Is that pussy still soaked for me?"

She clenched and more of our juices spilled from her. Her eyes were hooded, and I knew she wasn't done. She had more cum for me, I just had to reach forward and take it from her.

And I would.

I moved our fingers down between her legs, watching as she gasped when we hit her clit. We rounded it a few times before I dipped four of our fingers into her stretched, sensitive pussy.

She cried out, her brown eyes going wide, and I watched as her teeth met her lip, biting my own to fight the urge to take her mouth.

Not yet.

I dipped our fingers in and out, coating them in cum. She moaned and leaned further into me, and I felt my chest swell at the thought of being the man that was making her delirious.

I pulled our fingers free of her and smiled, feeding my coated digits to her.

"Suck."

Grabbing her wet fingers, I pulled them into my mouth, the creamy taste of us hitting my tongue.

"That's it," I said, watching her greedily suck and lick my fingers, bobbing her head.

I moaned as I swirled my tongue around her cum-soaked fingers.

I pulled my fingers from her mouth, capturing it with my own. Her lips were swollen and warm and I intended to fall into them.

My tongue ravaged her mouth.

I wanted to steal the very breath from her lungs. I wanted to be the only thing that she breathed, so she could feel this, feel how crazy she made me.

Grabbing her nipple, I greedily sucked her tongue. I swallowed every moan and groan as I squeezed and twisted, knowing that this gorgeous woman could take it. Take all the desire, all the darkness. When I pulled away, my lungs were burning, and we were both breathing hard.

My dick laid thick and heavy against her thigh. She reached for me, but I grabbed her hand and placed it on her thigh. I needed to know more about what she liked, how she fucked herself when no one was watching.

"Show me how you make yourself cum, Denise."

I grabbed the chair behind me, pulled it up, and took a seat. Her gaze was stuck to my dick, still soaked in her juices. She was staring at it like it was going to take a bite out of her.

"I said, show me." Her red face got a little redder, and I smiled. She loved it when I made demands. The second the words were out of my mouth, her fingers dipped down between her folds.

"Good girl."

Denise leaned back in her seat so she could cross her legs. Another tell. She only did that when she was turned on. Was she thinking about it too? The way her pussy clenched around me, her walls rippling as she came over and over again on my dick? Her gaze dips over to her briefcase again, and her back straightened.

I gave her a well-practiced look and her posture changed. She knew I had gossip. Leaning forward, I whispered the secret I overheard when someone walked past me earlier.

"Gloria's out today. Someone said she's getting her nose done."

"No! Again?" she laughed, her fingers coming to cover her mouth. "She's going to end up looking like early 2000s MJ."

"Not 'Butterflies' Michael! *Invincible* was so slept on." I clutched my chest in faux-pain.

"Before you start, nothing you say will change my mind that *Dangerous* was the best MJ album. He may have blatantly ripped off the Cleveland Orchestra, but that one minute of Beethoven before 'Will You Be There' changed my life."

I rolled my eyes and she gasped in outrage.

"Of course, your favorite song is the one from *Free Willy*," I chuckled.

She held up her hand. "Lies. 'Keep the Faith' is my favorite. But that tour version of 'Dangerous'..."

I hissed, and so did she.

"I'll give you that. Him with nothing but the snaps and the stomps." I shook my head. MJ was a bad man for that.

"Yes," she shouted.

Her excitement filled me with something. I didn't know what. I watched as she twirled in her seat.

"I figure we could grab lunch at eleven?" I crossed a leg over my knee and saw her wince. I tried to keep my eyes on the window and not on her, giving her the space to open up.

Both of our offices overlooked the city, with her view being a little smaller than mine.

"I wish I could, I have an appointment in SoMa," she said, after a moment. I could hear her indecision. She was trying to decide how much to share with me. I let her think it through, watching a far-off boat cutting slowly through the water as it headed toward the wharf.

Placing my hands in my lap, I brought my gaze to hers and remained quiet. She tried to avoid eye contact, absently scrolling on her computer, but the tension was dripping from her pores. After a few seconds, she sighed.

Without a word, she fished around in her briefcase and pulled out a small jewelry box.

A ring box.

Denise placed it between us gently like it was a ticking bomb.

It was like the room had suddenly turned into the Alaskan wilderness.

My body went cold.

I'd fucked up and waited too long, she was going to marry him.

A bead of sweat dripped down my spine and I straightened my back and hoped the fear didn't show on my face as I opened the box.

It was hideous. A blinding, ugly ring that no woman would ever willingly put on their finger. The center stone was massive and surrounded by smaller diamonds. Large baguette stones sat horizontally alongside the middle stones, and even more stones sat around those. I tugged it up and shook my head, closing the lid shut.

Maybe there *was* hope.

I showed her body what it was missing, and now this dipshit was showing her brain that he didn't know her. If I was proposing to Denise, I'd give her something modern, inspired by all those fantasy shows she never stops talking about. A solitaire cut, the band covered in green stones with a wedding band that fit across the top, resembling a crown.

I bit my cheek, cursing myself for falling into the dream.

This woman wasn't mine. Thinking about her that way was a recipe for disaster.

I slid it back over to her and said the only thing that felt right to say at that moment.

"It's not the right size."

The ring was tiny and Denny wasn't. She was soft and abundant. Every part of her moved and danced. Watching her laugh, truly laugh, was like watching the universe come to life. He didn't see what I saw. She was light and life and energy. And her goddamn ring finger wasn't a fucking size five.

Thinking about this ring in the right size on her finger made my chest tight. She couldn't marry him. I think she knew that she just needed to see it for herself.

My fingers crossed neatly into my lap before I asked the only real question worth asking. The question that would get me to stop chasing her, to put up my walls, to let her go.

"Are you happy?"

I took her off guard. Her lips pursed for a second before she replied.

"Of course not."

We stared at each other, the weight of what she'd just said sitting heavy between us. She caught herself off-guard, but I already knew. She hadn't been happy as long as I'd known her, not really.

I stood, needing to leave before I demanded she see reason.

"Are you happy? With Char?" Her words were whispered, and she looked surprised that she'd asked. I said the words I'd wanted to say to her for weeks.

I replied, just as softly, "Of course, I wasn't. That's why I left her."

That was all I could take before turning and walking away from her without looking back.

There was still a chance. Still, an opportunity to find my way to her, and I clung to that.

CHAPTER 4
DENISE

I left a few minutes after Hugh did. Partially because I couldn't focus on anything, but mostly because I couldn't get past the fact that everything was a mess.

Curtis came out for a moment last night to grab food, but didn't say a word to me before heading back into the spare room and closing the door behind him. It was the usual routine. I'd watch TV or read, and he'd be in the other room doing whatever until he needed something from me. He slept there; I slept in the bedroom.

While I was lying in bed trying to fall asleep, I went to the jewelry store's website and made an appointment. The only option for the next few days was today at lunch. I'd spent the last few hours running through all the ways I could ask the associate to swap the awful thing out.

Of course, I wasn't, that's why I left her.

He'd left Char and hadn't told me. What did that mean? Was I just reading into it, or did he think that wasn't supposed to raise a million questions?

Distaste for the ring was etched all over Hugh's face, which made me wonder what he would pick for me. I shook the thought away. My brain was making more problems for me, and I could barely manage the ones I already had.

The walk went by quickly and all too soon I stood in front of Johnson and Sons Family Jewelry.

This place was legendary for its craftsmanship and attention to detail. A few of their pieces literally took my breath away on their website. It was also Elizabeth Taylor's first stop whenever she was in the city. At least, that's what the plaque outside the building read. A tourist was snapping a photo with it as I weaved around them and headed toward the door.

Like most places in the city, there were bars across the windows to deter thieves and a burly man was standing inside the door, watching the few customers inside.

A voice piped through a speaker next to me before I could hit the buzzer.

"Good morning! Do you have an appointment?" The tinny voice came through the speaker.

I nodded and realized she probably couldn't see me, "Yes, an eleven for Denise."

"Perfect. Come on in," she said. A soft buzz was followed by a click and the door popped opened.

I stepped inside and took in the opulent store. The entire place was shiny and smelled like lavender. It was all happy reds and golds, and there were rows of all kinds of jewelry lining the walls. A quick look at the display cases didn't show any price tags. Okay, this place was *fancy* fancy. Nerves fluttered in my stomach. I'd never get over being in places like this.

"Afternoon." The guard said, his eyes fell quickly to my ass, and I smirked to myself. Even in a swanky place like this, leave it to men to do what they do.

A gorgeous older black woman with a short bob waved at me, and I breathed a sigh of relief as I walked up to her, smiling. It always gave me a thrill when I saw another sister in a fancy place. It was like an unwritten rule for us to smile and acknowledge the presence of one another.

"Hi there, I'm Sherry. What brings you in this lovely morning?" Sherry was standing ramrod straight as she looked at me across from a case full of diamond earrings.

"Hi Sherry, I'm Denny. Girl, I have a dilemma." I reached into my bag and pulled out the ring box, placing it down on the counter. I lowered my voice a bit before I continued.

"My boyfriend just bought this for me. I wanted to know what my options are." I placed as much emphasis on options as I could, hoping that she'd say there was an option for returns.

Sherry looked down at the box and her smile faltered a bit.

"He just bought this?" she asked.

"Yep, that's what he said."

She gently opened the box and pulled out the ring, turning it left and right before placing it back inside and closing the lid.

"I'll bring you over here, if that's okay," she said, walking to her right.

I followed her to a desk in the corner of the room. She placed the box on the desk and moved her seat around to sit closer to me, which I thought was odd until she opened her mouth.

"I need to be real with you."

Confused, I nodded. She covered my hand for a second before continuing.

"There's no way that he bought this here last week. We stopped working with this ring box in the nineties."

I looked from her to the box as she opened it, my stomach sinking to the floor as mortification heated my skin. Curtis lied to me?

"It's stamped PT, but this number is wrong. It should say 950 or 999. This says 925. But, before either of us jump to any conclusions, can I test the stones?"

I nod again and watched her grab the tester. She switched it on and leaned closer, keeping her voice soft, but pointed.

"This measures the thermal conductivity of the stone. If it is a diamond, it will beep."

She pressed the tip to the center stone and the indicator didn't move.

"Wait," I said, finally starting to comprehend the words. "The whole thing is fake."

"925 is the percentage for sterling silver. These stones are not diamonds. This box—" Before she could finish, I started to laugh. And I don't mean deranged, cute little giggles. I was belly laughing, holding my chest to ease the pressure because I couldn't breathe. It took me a good minute or two to get it out of my system.

Sherry was very concerned and had grabbed a box of tissues, thinking that I was going to lose my shit.

"If it helps, I've seen it before. Men can be trifling," she said, handing me a tissue.

I wiped at my tearing eyes and took a few deep breaths to compose myself.

"Of course you have, and of course he did." My heart was thudding in my chest, emotions that I couldn't even name were rolling around my head. I wanted to jump out of my skin to escape them.

Of course, was becoming a chorus in my head. Of course, he lied. Of course, he couldn't afford anything in this store. Of course, he chose something hideous. Of course, he didn't know me. We hadn't had a real conversation or touched each other in years. Of. Course.

Despite it all, I was relieved. A chilly wave wrapped itself tightly around me and made me feel numb. I knew it was going to be short-lived, but I welcomed it because this wasn't the place to process anything.

Sighing, I stood up and shoved the ring and box back into my bag.

"I—have to get back to work. I know it's weird. But, thank you." I whispered. She didn't have to pull me aside so discreetly. For that reason alone, I was never going to buy jewelry anywhere else.

"Yeah, girl, of course."

"The next time you see me, I'm getting these earrings you have on." I watched as the pear-shaped diamonds glimmered in the light.

Sherry pulled out a business card and slid it into my briefcase.

"Call me, I'll get you a good deal. Also, call me if you need to talk."

I felt my eyes start to tear and I cleared my throat, forcing them back. Sherry was a good one.

"I will." I smiled at her and headed back out the door, thankful that I had a few hours to figure out what the fuck my next steps were going to be before I went home.

CHAPTER 5
DENISE

My walk back to Foxx was a blur. I had planned to stop and grab a sandwich to eat at my desk, but I didn't even remember lunch until I was already walking back to my office. As I sat back down, I was eternally grateful that this was the lightest day of my week. It meant that I could sit and think and breathe.

Taking deep breaths, I found myself looking at my briefcase. Knowing what was in there made me want to chuck it off the roof.

The numbness had begun to fade and a calm, clear-headed rage was beginning to take its place. I imagined this is what the women on death row must feel right before they commit murder. Not blinding, passionate fury, but an eerily composed ferocity. I didn't know what I was going to do with that feeling, but I did know that I couldn't face Curtis feeling this way.

I pulled out my phone and texted Cleo, my partner in all things mischievous.

SOS.

Cleo messaged back almost immediately, and I snorted.

Who are we plotting to kill?

I replied with one word.

BITCH.

Her reply was immediate.

Say no more, I'll meet you at 6 with the flask.

Taking another deep breath, I did what I could to put my feelings in a box. I had a job to do, and I needed to stay sharp. There were a few emails from folks I needed to reply to and then I had to get started on my pet project: an upcycling furniture startup.

I spent the next half an hour stalking someone that I knew would be a great fit for these founders. They needed a seed investor who truly understood the value of mass-market furniture that used what folks threw away. Before I could bring this startup to anyone, I had to make sure I had all my ducks in a row.

My day went on like that, me throwing work on top of my stress, until I got a ping on my chat that I had a visitor downstairs that I hadn't signed in. The clock read six and I felt like an even bigger jerk. I'm sure Cleo had messaged my cell, but I'd put it on silent.

Shit.

I typed a quick message back to the front desk to let them know I'd meet her down in the lobby in a second as

I started throwing stuff into my briefcase. Part of being in this fancy-schmancy ass place was tight security. If Cleo wasn't on the guest list for today, she wouldn't be allowed up. Even if they did let her up on her own, someone would need to open the door for her with a different key card.

Cleo was used to me forgetting about her downstairs. Getting drunk on a work night wasn't unusual for us. I thanked my anxious brain for leaving a few outfits in her closet. We could get loaded and set up a plan.

I needed something concrete and written down before I confronted Curtis. Maybe even a prepared statement that I printed and read out loud to make sure I was saying all the things I needed to say. And a space without any sharp objects, lest I lose my mind and throw one at his face.

I was looking back at my desk to make sure I had gotten everything as I ran out the door and right into someone.

It was Hugh.

Of course, it was Hugh. His cologne today was musky and sweet. I somehow managed to keep my hands off him as he steadied me.

"In a hurry?" His voice did things to me. I bit my lip, knowing that he didn't mean it the way that my body was interpreting it. Not after this morning.

"A little," I admitted.

He was quiet and so was I. I didn't know what to say and as much as I willed my feet to walk away, I couldn't do it.

Finally looking up to meet his eyes, it was clear that Hugh felt the same way. Something unspoken was flowing between us—

"Deeds!" The screech came from the front door, and Hugh lifted a quizzical brow while I covered my face.

"How did she get up here?" I muttered, turning to see Cleo half-dancing toward me with a bashful Bill walking behind her.

"Bill," Hugh said, nodding.

Bill, the security guard from downstairs, half-waved, probably because what he'd done was totally against the rules. He looked between us and his eyebrows went up. I rolled my eyes as he laughed.

Cleo wobbled a bit. She'd clearly started drinking without me. She caught sight of Hugh and her smile nearly split her face in two. Double shit.

"Hey Bill, I've got her, thanks for bringing her up," I said, grabbing Cleo's hand and dragging her next to me.

"She's very persistent," Bill said, starting to walk backward. "Have a lovely night, ladies. And Hugh." Bill winked as he left.

I turned to see Cleo staring at Hugh.

"Yahweh." Cleo tilted up her chin.

I nearly choked on my spit, and I squeezed her hand tight, my eyes going wide as I looked at her.

"Cleo," Hugh said, smiling wide. I could hear the laughter and arrogance in his voice. I sighed.

"We were just on our way out."

Shoving Cleo, I tried to make a hasty exit, but she didn't budge. She handed me the cute flowery flask instead and I took a drink.

It wasn't until the liquid sloshed around in my stomach that I remembered it was empty. Good, that made it easier.

"I hope I'm not interrupting anything." The look in her eye told me that she did indeed hope she was interrupting something.

Hugh turned to look at me, his gaze was hooded and scalding.

"Nothing that we can't finish at a later time."

Heat crept up my neck as I bit my lip. Nope. I moved the flask back to my lips.

Cleo snatched it from me and took a long, exaggerated swig, while Hugh stepped forward, grabbing my bag from my hand and slowly sliding it up to my shoulder.

Leaning close, he whispered, "Be a good little menace, I'd hate to have to punish you later."

Warmth pooled low in my stomach as I squeaked before I could stop the sound from escaping my lips.

"Don't keep her out too late, it's a school night." Hugh winked before turning and sauntering back to his office.

"Bitch, are you blushing?" Cleo half-whispered. "Am *I* blushing?"

I didn't look, I just watched as Hugh's round ass bounced back into his office like he didn't just leave a pool in my panties. Little Menace... And I thought I liked being called a good girl.

Fuck me.

CHAPTER 6
DENISE

"I know you are absolutely lying to my motherfucking face right now, Denise."

Cleo was staring at the ring that she'd dropped on the table as I told her the story of my afternoon.

I was drunk.

The cream shirt I'd worn to work was on the ground somewhere. I was lying backward on her couch. The gorgeous red bra Hugh had bought for me secured around my chest. They were worth the huge price tag for that alone. All of my other bras would immediately be on the floor, kicked into a corner, the second I was out of public view but this one was comfy, hours later.

"You're sure? You're, like, super sure?" Cleo was just as drunk as I was, but her mood shifted the more I spoke.

I shrugged, throwing my hands out.

"The lady pressed the thing on it, and it was fake. Glass, cubic zirconia, whatever! And, like, if you were gonna spend thousands of dollars on a ring, wouldn't you steal one of the rings I already own and see that I wear a size nine? Look at me. Is there anything about me that hints that my ring size would be a five?!" I laughed to myself as the heat started to fill my face and my stomach roiled.

"Wait. I have an idea." She pulled out her phone.

Placing the ring back in the box, she snapped a photo of it and smiled.

"Reverse image search."

I jumped up off the couch and put out my hand, dizzy as shit. Swallowing against the sweaty feeling in the back of my throat, I took a second to let myself settle.

Hint taken, don't drunkenly hang upside down.

"Oh. Fuck," she whispered.

I clambered over her coffee table and sat beside her.

There it was.

The exact ring on a website boasting about how close it looked to the real thing.

"Fifty bucks." She breathed, looking at me and grabbing my wrist.

Nine years of my life. Fifty dollars.

I started laughing again. This time, tears burned behind my eyes. Wiping at them angrily, I threw my head back against the couch.

Cleo laid her head in my lap and sighed while I tried to control the riot of emotions running through my head.

"This is so shitty. I was ready. I came home ready to end it." I closed my eyes as I pressed my palms against them.

"And you thought the ring changed something?" Cleo asked.

"I did. For a second, I thought maybe..." I stopped, sighing.

"Maybe what?"

"Maybe I'd gotten it all wrong. I fucked up with Hugh and Curtis just needed time to get his shit together."

Cleo squeezed my calf.

"And now? Knowing that he lied?"

I started to rub my eyes again.

"I feel like an idiot. Like, I let this all happen to me." I blew out a breath and looked down at Cleo. She was giving me the saddest smile and that made me feel even worse. Cleo wasn't the sad smile type, she was who you came to when you needed to laugh.

"It's not all bad. I mean, remember that time your cat died, and he told you to stop crying because it wasn't a big deal?" Cleo rolled her eyes and sucked her teeth.

I knew she was doing her thing and trying to cheer me up, but, that moment, that exact moment, was when things changed between Curtis and me.

We didn't truly understand one another and as much as I fought for him, changed for him, we were never the same. He was a country boy who grew up in an almost all-white town and I was from LA. It was never going to work.

Deep down, I'd known it was over after that fight. I'd just accepted unhappiness.

I couldn't do it, not anymore.

Pushing Cleo off me, I grabbed my phone and walked toward my shirt.

"Okay, maybe don't think about when your cat died," she said, watching me throw the shirt over my head.

"I'll be right back."

Cleo lived a quick five minutes from my apartment. Even though I'd told myself that I wasn't going home tonight, my drunk brain said it was now or never.

I needed to get this off my chest and it had to be brutal and honest. There was no coming back for Curtis and me, and he needed to accept that.

"Wait." Cleo was up and standing in front of me as I threw on my shoes. "Maybe this is a sober conversation?"

Reaching past her, I grabbed the ring and shoved it in my pocket.

"Nope. It's a right-now conversation."

"Shit, hold on." Cleo ran to grab her shoes and threw them on as I flung open the door to the apartment.

"I said hold on! Damn!" I heard Cleo call out behind me, but I was already making for her stairs, taking them carefully and one at a time. Drunk didn't mean stupid. I'd already almost thrown up, I didn't want to make a pair of crutches my newest fashion accessory.

When I pushed through the door, I heard Cleo running behind me.

"Take your coat, you silly bitch." She threw it over my shoulders, and I put it on.

We walked in silence for a second before Cleo started talking.

"So, what's the plan?"

"You mean other than telling him to get his shit and get out?" I threw my head back and looked up as my breath clouded and floated up. It was a clear and breezy night. The city lights erased most of the stars, but I preferred the inky black void that I'd grown up seeing.

The stars made everything feel too big sometimes. I think they were a reminder I was stuck standing in the same place no matter how far I went. They also made me think of my dad, and that was something I definitely didn't need to think about right now.

"Tonight?" Cleo asked, shoving her hands into the pockets of her jacket.

"Depends on how it goes down, I guess. I may need to stay—"

"Oh, shut up. You know you can stay as long as you need to." Cleo sighed. "Are you sure about this? I'm not gonna stop you, but this is a lot, Den."

I thought about what she'd said. It *was* a lot. But I was holding tight to something that no longer existed.

For years, I'd been building a life on my own, I hadn't been building it with Curtis. When I first started at Foxx, he wanted me to stop working. He didn't see the value in what I did or the people that I helped. He wanted a version of me that was never going to exist.

Hell, I didn't even know which version of me I even was anymore.

I came home to someone I couldn't even talk to about my day because he didn't care. And I didn't ask about his day because I didn't care, either.

I needed to put us both out of our misery because this ring, the one burning a giant hole straight through my pocket, wasn't given out of love, it was from obligation. It was a precursor, the next step to something I didn't want, and a sign of what I didn't have with Curtis. I had to let him go.

We stopped outside my apartment building, and I grabbed Cleo's arm and hooked mine through hers.

"I'm sure."

We walked up the stairs together and stopped beside the door.

"Can you wait for me?" I asked, shrugging off my coat and handing it to her.

She gave me a look that said, *Duh, bitch,* and I let go of her elbow to open the apartment door. I went to close it but thought better of it, leaving it partially open, so I didn't have to repeat everything for Cleo later.

Curtis was awake and in his room with the door shut. I could hear the muffled sounds of whatever game he was playing and the soft sound of music.

I opened the door. Curtis didn't look up from the screen, but his headphones were slightly askew. I knew he had heard me.

"Curtis, we need to talk," I said, my voice surprisingly even and somber.

"I'm in the middle of someth—"

"It's about Ruby." Nope, that wasn't right. Get it together, drunk brain.

Curtis looked briefly over at me before squinting. "Who?"

Of course, he didn't remember the name of my fucking cat. It had been years since we'd argued about her.

Rage began to boil beneath the skin of my cheeks, but I kept talking.

"The ring is too small," I said, changing subjects. Curtis still wasn't looking at me, his fingers were dancing across keys as he kept his gaze on his monitor.

"On your left, yeah, I got him," he said into the microphone at his lips. He had the nerve to flick his hand at me without looking. "Leave it, I'll get it fixed or whatever."

"I stopped by the jeweler, Curtis."

He startled, looking over at me before glancing back at his computer. His lips thinned before he said, "Oh, can they resize it, I have the rec—"

"Stop lying! Why would you keep lying?" I yelled.

He paled, looking nervous as he started fidgeting with his computer. "Wait—"

"Ruby was my cat. Of course you don't remember? 'It's just a cat, Denise, stop crying.' That's what you said."

His face squished together as he turned to me and pulled off his headphones, "It *was* just a cat, and you were being ridiculous!"

"No. I was grieving a pet I'd had for twenty years!"

"Jesus Christ, it was on death's door for months. Was I supposed to pretend I was shocked that it croaked?!"

"Oh, but you'll pretend this thing is fucking real!" I pulled the ring from my pocket. "This is a lie. It's disgusting. *You* are disgusting."

I threw it at him. "Even if it was real. Even if you had asked me, I would've said no."

"Denise, watch how you talk—" He was getting angry.

"Or what?" I leaned close to him and laughed. "Exactly. Your threats are just like your promises... empty."

Curtis stood, his chest heaving.

"Get the fuck out of my house. Return that shitty ring. Maybe then your broke ass will have some money for a bus ticket back to Nebraska."

I turned to leave and got halfway to the door before Curtis grabbed my upper arm in a bruising grip and pulled me backward.

"You can't just leave." His fingers were digging deeper and deeper into my skin.

"Watch me." I yanked my arm, but he pulled me back towards him.

"Get off of me," I screamed, my free hand slapping the shit out of him.

"No!" Curtis barely reacted as he shook me, moving to grab my other arm, and I kicked out, hitting his upper thigh. My fist was balled up, ready to punch him, when I heard the door slam into the wall. Cleo ran in, shoulder first, and threw all of her substantial weight into his chest.

Falling back, his nails scratched deep into my flesh as he hit the floor. I stumbled with him, letting out a pained yelp, as I fought to stay upright.

Taking advantage, Cleo grabbed her keychain and unloaded a can of mace in his face. My eyes and nose stung from the scent of it.

Curtis howled, holding his eyes, and blindly reached around the room.

Cleo pushed me out, slamming the door behind us as he screamed. She started pulling me towards the front door, but I pulled back.

"I need to pack my stuff," I said, running toward the bedroom.

"Right now?! Bitch, we gotta go." Cleo ran behind me as I grabbed two suitcases from the top of the closet.

"You saw him. Would you leave him in a room with all the shit you cared about?" I started throwing everything I could into one of the suitcases.

Cleo disappeared for a second and came back with a giant kitchen knife.

"This means diddly squat if the country bumpkin has a gun. And If I get shot defending you while you pack a bunch of bullshit, you are going to owe me tequila for the rest of my life. And a kidney. Maybe a piece of your liver too."

I didn't really look at what I was grabbing, I just grabbed what I could reach and zipped it shut. I put everything, hangars and all, into the second suitcase as we heard movement in the other room.

"Hurry up," Cleo hissed, staring daggers at the closed door.

I zipped the second bag shut and dragged it forward as Cleo pulled the other.

As the office door jerked open, I let out a small squeal. A red and puffy-faced Curtis was splashing a water bottle over his head.

Cleo was holding my jacket and the knife as she stood by my side. We slowly backed up toward the open apartment door.

He glared at me as Cleo pulled me back through the doorway.

"Leave, or I'm calling the cops," I said, sounding stronger than I felt.

I closed the door and blinked away tears, feeling the blood flowing down to my wrist chilling against my skin.

What the fuck.

CHAPTER 7
DENISE

I spent most of my day in the office with the door closed. Hugh had walked past a few times, but I nodded my head and returned to my work. I needed the distraction. I couldn't think, I couldn't breathe without feeling like I was going to fly into a rage or cry. I'd barely slept, I was hungover and exhausted, and as much as I wanted to be anywhere but here, I felt safest here. At work. In a place where everything was familiar, and the days looked the same.

It was eighty degrees in my office with the sun beating on my back, but I kept my blazer on. I'd taken one look at my arm this morning and knew I had to cover it.

Someone knocked and opened the door. Not just any someone, it was Lucian Foxx. I blinked, confused.

Lucian was standing in my doorway. It would probably be more apt to say the man *became* my doorway.

Lucian was six-foot-five, I'd never seen him wear anything that looked dark and brooding. Today, his suit was a light gray that contrasted well against his caramel skin. If that wasn't enough to get your attention, his sharp eyes were an icy cobalt blue. Blue enough that when he dressed up as a white walker last Halloween, I steered clear of him all night because it freaked me out.

"Do you have a moment?" It wasn't a real question, but I nodded anyway.

"Yes, sir," I said.

Lucian started walking without looking back. I jumped up and speed walked forward, catching him entering Hugh's office.

My heart thudded in my chest, but I followed him in.

Lucian sat on the couch and gestured for me to close the door. I placed a suddenly sweaty palm against the door. Lucian had said three words to me the whole time I had worked for him. He hadn't even called me into his office when I got my promotion, he'd emailed me asking me to update my email signature.

This was either very good or awful.

Hugh moved to stand beside me. I couldn't look at him. I took a deep breath. If this was about us, the HR rep would be here. I tried to calm my racing heart by taking a deep breath.

Lucian pulled out his phone and started typing away with long fingers. We stood silently, waiting for him to speak.

I repeated *this is fine* over and over in my head, but that didn't stop the familiar shivering from flowing through my body. I was starting to feel like I couldn't catch my breath.

No, not now.

"Denise, you've been doing an amazing job with the interns. I know you've only been a Principal for a year, but I want to see if you have what it takes to be a Partner. I am emailing you both this quarter's strongest pitches. Pick one and run it—start to finish."

Hugh's computer pinged as Lucian stood and looked at me. Partner work? I didn't even have my own team yet and I was being considered for Partner? I felt like my body was underwater.

"Any questions?"

I shook my head as my neck started to heat underneath my collar. Hugh made a quiet noise next to me and I spoke, "No, sir. Thank you for this opportunity. I'm looking forward to finding the perfect enterprise organization worthy of Foxx."

Lucian nodded and turned his attention to Hugh, "I'll let the team know at our meeting later." He strolled out of the room and shut the door behind him.

I took a short breath and then another, staring at the door. The flush crept up into my scalp and I felt like I was going to combust.

"Denny," Hugh said. He sounded far away, too far away.

I waved him off and walked over to his couch and fell on it. I was already emotionally raw, and the idea of being reprimanded tipped me over the edge.

I don't do this.

I don't make decisions on a whim.

And Curtis. Curtis scared the shit out of me last night.

Was I really going to call the cops on him if he didn't leave? Was it even worth it to file a report against him for grabbing me? Cleo was there, but she was also my friend.

What if no one believed me...

Everything was falling apart. Each piece of my life was slipping through my fingers, and I couldn't hold everything together and take on more work on top of it all. My head was swimming. I started to feel lightheaded.

"Denny?"

I barely heard him, my attention was on the view. My breaths started to come faster. It dawned on me that I really did want this job. Extravagance aside, I was helping people's dreams come true. I was. But my dreams were all shattered, fragmented and broken. What did I want? Who was I trying to be?

Hugh leaned down next to me, his face coming into view.

"Breathe with me."

Was I not breathing? I felt like I was breathing. I was breathing a lot. Too much. My chest was heavy and things were blurring.

My hands were placed on something warm, but my gaze was still on the skyline. It was foggy and gray today.

"Denise." Hugh snapped at me.

His tone caught my attention, dragging me back to the fact that my heart felt like it was beating out of my chest. My lungs were seizing. I felt my vision starting to dim.

"Focus on me and breathe." He was using that no-nonsense tone, with his hand under my chin. His touch broke through the waves of anxiety currently drowning me, and I furrowed my brow as his hand squeezed my cheeks together.

"Do what I said."

I took a shuddering short breath.

"Another."

I gulped in more air, feeling my lungs fighting hard against me with every inhale. I wanted to cry, to succumb to the inky black that was edging my vision. The pain was coiled tight in my chest. Another breath, another.

I lost count of how many breaths I took before the blur coating my vision faded, and the tightness coiled in my chest began to ease.

When the breaths came a little easier, I realized my hands were against Hugh's chest.

His steady heartbeat thumped against my palms as I started to feel tension draining from my shoulders. Tears clouded my vision and I tried and failed to blink them back.

"That's it. Good." Hugh wiped my cheeks, keeping his eyes on mine.

"Let's take this off." He reached for the edges of my blazer. I moved to take my hands back.

"I'm fine," I said, panic rising again. He couldn't find out. I didn't want anyone to know.

"Okay. Okay," Hugh whispered. "Just sit here for a minute. Stay here with me."

We sat together, me breathing deep as Hugh's sharp gaze came into focus. My fingers felt every rise and fall of Hugh's chest until my breaths matched his.

"What do you need?" Hugh asked.

A time machine.

World peace.

Him.

"My purse—"

"I got it. I'll be right back." Hugh left me alone and I covered my face.

Each breath I took helped ease the panic, while also making me feel more and more embarrassed.

A panic attack. At work. In front of Hugh.

He came back with my purse in hand and a bottle of water. I didn't meet his gaze as I rummaged around and found the pill bottle. Snapping one in half, I put it under my tongue and scrunched my nose as it dissolved. I downed the whole bottle of water when it was done.

Hugh sat beside me. After a moment, his hand went to the nape of my neck and pulled me gently to his shoulder.

Before I could stop them, more tears fell. I wiped at them and sniffed.

"Sorry. Thanks. Sorry," I mumbled.

The comedown was the worst part.

Being thrown in and out of fight or flight floods everything with adrenaline and is emotionally and physically exhausting.

Hugh placed his chin on my head.

"I'm glad I was here," Hugh said.

So was I. This felt good, *he* felt good. I felt tears building again, but I blinked them back.

Hugh was everything I needed. The realization hit me like a sack of potatoes to the face.

That was the other thing about my panic attacks, they usually came with some lightbulb moment of realization that my brain couldn't comprehend until it was soaked in adrenaline.

The first time I'd had a panic attack, I was thirteen. I started hyperventilating over graduation as I realized my father was never coming back home. That I'd never see him again. I passed out in the middle of the lunchroom. I'd had a lot since then, but none around other people.

Hugh held me as I fought the urge to relax into him. We were blurring the line. I couldn't saddle him with all my shit, that's not what he signed up for.

"I'm going to try and take a cat nap before the staff meeting."

I needed to get out, to get away from him, away from everyone.

Sleep sounded like the perfect way to reset my brain. If it wasn't for Lucian dropping this project on us, I'd have gone home. But how bad would it look if the billion-dollar man gave me the opportunity of a lifetime and I just left? No, I had to suck it up. I could do this.

I stood and Hugh stood with me.

When I reached down to grab my bag, Hugh grabbed my hand and brought it to his mouth, placing a kiss against my palm.

"Thank you for being vulnerable with me," he whispered.

Unexpectedly, my stomach somersaulted once and then twice. Before I could think better of it, my fingers moved to his cheek, feeling the coarseness of his beard beneath my touch.

"Thank you for letting me be vulnerable," the words were barely there, but I meant them. Maybe I was wrong.

Maybe he wanted to be this for me, not out of obligation, but because he cared.

If I wasn't careful, I was going to get addicted to this man. Something told me I'd never get him out of my system if I did.

CHAPTER 8
DENISE

The staff meeting was—awkward... The whole team was crowded in the lobby as Lucian spoke. Thankfully, the man was eighteen feet tall, so everyone got a good look at him as he announced that Hugh and I were partnering on the new H1 client. I was glad the nap had worked because standing there was uncomfortable. I could hear a few whispers among the crowd, speculating and gossiping about the scandalous turn of events.

It was Xavier's job. The Chief Operating Partner had been doing it for as long as I'd been at Foxx and probably long before I arrived.

I looked over at Xavier in a dated banker-blue suit. He was trying his best not to look aggrieved as all one hundred people in the office glanced in his direction. He didn't say a word and he didn't have to. The rage in his eyes was clear and pretty scary.

Once Lucian changed the conversation to holiday schedules and PTO, I happened to look over at Xavier and saw him bouncing his murderous gaze toward Hugh and then me. I tried to ignore it, but after the fifth time, I glanced up and found myself looking right at him.

I don't know if it was the bitch in me, the power nap I'd just taken, or the Zen drugs flowing through me, but I gave him a little finger wave. His face turned beet red, and I bit my lip to stop the smile, turning my attention back to the HR lead talking. Thankfully, that was the last agenda item.

As we all started to walk back to our desks, I saw Hugh heading right for me. Uh oh.

"Your office."

He led the way, and I followed behind him, confused.

I watched as he shut the door firmly behind me and narrowed his eyes.

"Tell me you're high. Are you high?"

My face must've shown my confusion because he continued.

"He could destroy you and you're taunting him?"

I scoffed. "Oh, I think you're being a bit dramatic."

"Xavier isn't some nobody, he's got half of the Saint Francis Yacht Club on speed dial," Hugh said, dropping the name of the most exclusive club in the city.

"I am pretty sure they don't say the full name like that."

Hugh glared at me and kept talking like he hadn't heard me.

"Lucian just shit all over him in front of the entire office. I don't want you stuck in the middle of some power play between those two."

Hugh was already a Partner. In fact, most folks considered him a better COP than Xavier. Hugh closed more deals than him and could wrap a whole room around his finger with a smile and a joke.

This wasn't the first time I'd been talked at by Hugh. Whenever he felt like I wasn't toeing the corporate line enough, he'd tell me so. And as much as it annoyed me, he was almost always right.

I stepped forward and kicked the edge of his shoe with mine. It was a ploy to see how mad he was. He toed my shoe back and I smiled. Medium mad. I could work with that.

"We're already in it, Hugh," I gently reminded him.

"We are," he agreed, looking up, "but we don't have to play it that way."

"You're right. I know you're right," I relented, watching his features relax.

"Thank you," he said.

"He still started it, though." I shrugged.

I expected him to start chiding me again. Instead, Hugh leaned back against the front of my desk, smiling.

"You're feeling better."

It wasn't a question. But he was right. The nap helped focus my post-anxiety attack clarity. But it wasn't *just* the nap. It was him.

Hugh was giving me all the things I knew I'd needed and settled on not having. As horrible as last night had been, it was nice to think about something else and fold back into Work Denny. And as crazy as things were becoming at Foxx, I didn't have to worry about Curtis and sending him money anymore.

I could focus solely on myself.

This was a golden opportunity to work hard and show Lucian that I was capable of more. I was ready to really pour myself into work and my career. Everything else could follow along after.

"Are you looking for a thank you?" I raised my eyebrows and cleared my throat. "You didn't take me as the type that needed attention."

I was deflecting. We both knew it. Instead of calling me on it, he tilted his head.

"If there wasn't a room full of people outside, I'd fuck that smug look right off your face." His voice deepened and he kept up that smile, but the innocence in it was gone.

A blush crept up my neck. I looked down and saw his pants were tighter than before.

If anyone was looking in, it would look like a normal conversation. They wouldn't see the way his eyes brightened or my breaths coming quicker.

All they'd see was the smile on his face and his hands innocently tucked into his pockets.

"You can't chastise me for being reckless when you clearly enjoy seeing it." The offense I injected into my tone sounded fake, even to my ears.

He looked deep in thought for a moment before biting his lip and crossing his feet in front of him.

"Tell me you don't enjoy coming on my tongue."

I tried to pretend like my pussy didn't clench at the thought, and I cleared my throat. It was time to play my trump card.

"Actually, I have a question," I said, a smile playing on my lips.

Hugh didn't reply. I kept talking.

"I've been thinking about it, and I have to know," I left a dramatic pause, "which of your clients was asking about me?"

Hugh's gaze darkened and I smiled sweet and bright.

"The idea of becoming some rich man's kept woman—"

Hugh moved forward quicker than I expected. He had my back against the door while his hand grabbed at my neck and squeezed. A flash of pressure gave way to pleasure, and I bit my cheek to stop the moan from escaping my lips.

"Not an option," Hugh whispered against my lips as his hand tightened on my throat.

"You're sure?" I was egging him on, daring him to keep going and relishing in the haze of desire that was flooding through me.

"I have the perfect cure for that mouth, and it's not my dick. That's a reward you have to earn."

A wave of heat rolled through me again, laying heavily between my legs. I turned to look out my window and realized the blinds were still drawn from my nap. Hugh tightened his hold.

"No. You look at me."

My gaze came back to his as I felt the peaks of my nipples brushing against my blazer and I tried to get on my tippy-toes to relieve the pressure, but he just followed my movements. His tongue snuck out, tasting my lips as he grazed his nose against mine.

He loosened his hand, smiling as I took one deep breath after another.

"You were saying?" His hand ran down my injured arm. I hissed as his touch dragged my blazer across the raw skin.

"What—" he looked at me, confused, and I averted my gaze.

All the pleasure he'd stoked fell away, and I was cold all over again. The confusion and then understanding on his face opened a pit below me, obliterating the ease I'd gotten from my nap.

I pushed at Hugh and tried to walk past him to my desk.

"Take it off." He held my hand and he spoke using that tone—the one that made bigwigs open their wallets and caused entire rooms to sit up straight.

I shook my head, avoiding eye contact and trying to change the subject.

"Hugh—"

"Denise. Take off the fucking blazer."

CHAPTER 9
HUGH

Denise was scared. Something was up, and there was no fucking way I was leaving this office until she told me the goddamn truth. And she was going to start by taking off that blazer and showing me why she hissed the second I touched her arm.

She'd known me for too long to fool herself into thinking that I was going to let this go. I was standing here as long as it took. I made sure she could hear it in my voice and see it in my eyes.

Her eyes went round and glassy. Without a word, she grabbed the edge of her sleeve, pulling her arm free with a wince, sliding the blazer free from her shoulders.

Blotchy purple and blue bruises marked her skin, almost glowing in the fluorescent lighting. I worked hard to hide my rage as I spotted four deep scratches across the bruises, freshly scabbed and an angry crimson.

She laid her blazer on the desk as I stepped forward and turned her arm closer to the natural light. He'd done this. I knew it. He'd hurt her and I was going to rip his fucking balls off.

My years in corporate America had given me the best poker face in the business. I could hate your fucking guts and you wouldn't have a clue. I was using every muscle, every inch of my being not to show the utter rage flowing under my skin. The desire to march across the city and destroy Curtis was dizzying.

But, before I could do that, I had to take care of my girl.

Mine.

I wasn't waiting for her to choose me. I was choosing for her.

My fingers gently grabbed her palm as I turned her arm left and right. Swallowing hard against the lump in my throat, my fingers found her chin.

"Are you okay?"

She shrugged, leaning back onto her desk. I knew this Denny. She didn't want to talk, she felt like showing me this made her weak. This woman. This fucking woman. *Breathe*, Hugh.

"What do you need?"

It was the second time I'd asked that question today. The first was in my office earlier.

I knew she had a panic disorder, but it was the first time I'd ever seen her have an attack. It had scared the shit out of me at first, but once I got her to focus, she was able to take her control back.

But this was different. This wasn't about getting her to breathe and calm her heart rate. She was hurt and afraid. I couldn't fix the hurt, but I could fix the fear.

She walked around her desk and sat down, opening up her email.

"I need to work," she said.

Fuck work.

I frowned but kept my voice even. "Denise."

"It's—probably not even what you think." She stuttered on the lie.

"And what exactly do I think?" My tone was ice. I was standing so close to her, I could see her lip tremble as she struggled not to cry.

She reached out toward me, but she stopped herself. Her eyes were wide and for the first time, I could see how exhausted she was. Shame flashed across her face. I had to ball my fists to stop myself from reaching for her.

She took a breath and turned back to her computer.

"If the flirting is done and you're not planning on fucking me, you can go. I have a lot of work to do, and so do you." She was trying to match my tone, but the frost wasn't there, all I could hear was humiliation and pain.

Without acknowledging her words, I turned and walked out the door, shutting it behind me.

I pulled my phone from my pocket as I walked, opening LinkedIn, and navigating to my notifications to find Cleo's name. A few clicks showed me her website and I dialed the number and put the phone to my ear, shutting my office door.

"This is Cleo Johnson."

In any other circumstance, I'd have commented on her immaculate code-switching, but I didn't have time.

"It's Hugh. Did what I think happen last night?"

There was a long pause on her end before she answered.

"I maced him… How did you get my number?"

Of course, she maced him. I smiled at her question.

"If you're going to cyberstalk someone, you should set your settings to private," I teased.

"People can see when I look at them?!" The screech was blistering. I pulled the phone from my ear.

"Cleo. Let me help." It wasn't a question, I'm sure she heard that.

"He should be out tonight. Maybe you can swing by and change the locks?"

"Will do," I said, looking at my calendar and deciding which meetings I could push.

"Is she okay?" Cleo asked, her tone worried.

"She will be," I assured her.

I hung up the phone and saw Cleo had sent me Denise's address. I hoped to God that man was gone because if he wasn't...

My last meeting ran late. I'd hoped to get over to Denny's apartment by six, but it was after seven by the time I'd run to the store for a new doorknob and found my way to her complex. I could hear the sound of things breaking as I came up the stairs.

I took a minute to shrug off my coat and suit jacket and fold them over my arm.

The moron was still there.

I smiled.

Good.

The apartment door was half open and I heard what sounded like shattering glass.

Curtis was wearing filthy sweats, caked in food and makeup. The stench of chemicals was overwhelming. I watched as he emptied a bottle of red wine all over the couch, his back to me.

I took a slow and deep breath, trying to tamp down the fury of seeing this sorry excuse for a man destroying the place he'd laid his head. As he pulled his arm back to throw the bottle, I saw the state of the couch he'd destroyed. Had that asshole taken a knife to the—

Alright, he was fucking done.

"That's enough." My voice boomed against the walls of the apartment.

He screamed, dropping the bottle.

Coward.

"Who the fuck are you?"

I'd met Curtis twice before. It didn't surprise me that he had no clue who I was. He was a selfish prick. Case in point.

"You need to leave." I wasn't here to answer his questions, I was here to make sure he got the fuck out.

"Or what?" He was trying to be menacing, but I had at least seventy-five pounds on him. He took a few steps toward me. That was all the invitation I needed.

I gave him a blinding smile and dropped the bag in my hand to the ground, placing my jacket on the empty TV stand.

"Or I'll beat you like your bitch ass daddy should've."

Curtis made a strangled sound and took a swing at me. His gait was unsteady as he lunged toward me. Had this moron ever been in a fight before?

Moving sideways, I brought my fist into his stomach, right into his diaphragm. Watching him hunch over and struggle to breathe. I saw flashes of Denise's bruises as I brought my knee up to his face, listening for the telltale crack. Delicious.

He fell to the ground, his face bleeding. I didn't let his whimpering stop me. Dragging him across the floor, I made sure to cut a pathway through as much of the glass as I could. He kicked at me, and I dodged him, landing a kick of my own into his stomach. He reached for my leg, and I kicked him again and again. I wanted to mark him so he could wake up feeling the reminder of what a piece of fucking shit he was.

It felt good to see him bleeding. My mind went back to a different time. Looking at the kitchen counter above me, I saw a block of knives. It wasn't a switchblade, but it would do. I stood, reaching over to take a look at what I had to choose from.

Curtis had given up trying to fight back and was curled in on himself, whimpering. Like that would stop me. Knife in hand, I leaned down, the glass crunching beneath my feet.

I caught the tip of his chin with the chef's knife. He froze when he felt the cold steel biting into his skin. I tried to remember who I was now and not who I used to be. The blood was rushing in my ears, and I could see his lips moving, but I couldn't hear what he was saying.

"Twenty-five years ago, a switchblade would've dug into your rib cage, maybe finding its way into your lung or your liver." I put some pressure on the knife, my heart racing as blood began to drip down his neck.

The smell of piss hit my nose and my smile grew wilder.

"I'm gonna give you one more chance to get the fuck out of here before I forget the man I've become." I flipped the knife blade away from him and watched as he dragged himself up, glass glinting among the blood, as he scurried out of the door.

I dropped the knife to the ground and looked down at it. A smear of blood stained the edge. My chest constricted as I breathed against the rage flooding my body, the pull to chase him down and finish what I started. I grabbed for my suit jacket, feeling the wool beneath my fingers. Slipping it on, I stood in the open doorway, welcoming the chill and pulling the frigid air deep into my lungs.

I needed to remember.

Switch is gone. Dead. And. Buried.

CHAPTER 10
DENISE

It was almost eight-thirty, and I was finally eating dinner in Cleo's studio apartment. I'd spent the rest of my afternoon doing some precursory research on the list that Hugh and I had been sent. I did manage to whittle the list down, but we still had a long way to go. Hugh never replied to my message about working through dinner, so I just stayed on until I couldn't take the rumbling in my stomach anymore.

Thankfully, it was a Friday. With any luck I'd be sleeping through the entire weekend. That was definitely the plan tonight, the second the rest of this food was in my belly. Cleo's attention was bouncing from her phone to my arm, her face furious.

We hadn't said much to each other since this morning. She was upset that I refused to take the day off. I was glad she wasn't asking me anything. I didn't want to talk. I wanted to forget everything, just for tonight.

After I caught her looking for the fifth time, I couldn't take it anymore, "I'm fine. Eat. Please."

She shook her head, picked up her fork, and stabbed aggressively at her rice and I figured she was imagining she was stabbing Curtis.

Halfway through my enchiladas, my own phone buzzed on the table. Dread filled me as I saw that it was a text from Curtis. Swiping up, I read the text aloud.

"Keep the apartment. And tell your psycho friends I'll leave you the fuck alone. Have fun cleaning."

My heart sank. Cleaning? What did he do?

"Cleo." She was already standing and pocketing her phone. I looked over at the suitcases tucked behind her couch as she moved around them to grab her shoes.

"Grab your coat, Denny."

I waited for Cleo, this time, as we abandoned our dinners and made the walk back over to my place. Cleo hooked her arm into mine.

"Whatever it is, we can fix it," she said.

I nodded.

"And you got some stuff out. So, that's good."

I nodded again.

When we made it to my apartment, I saw that the door was open.

"If he's in here, I'm doing more than macing his ass this time," Cleo whispered, lifting the canister and her ginormous key ring.

Taking a steeling breath, I pushed open the door and took in a shocked breath. Hugh was sweeping up glass and flower petals surrounded by chaos.

The apartment was wrecked, pillows were slashed open and leaking fluff, food was spread across counters, and the pungent stench of bleach made my eyes water.

An already full trash bag sat to Hugh's right. And he'd just started filling up another.

"Hey," he said, broom in hand.

"What are you doing here?" I asked, looking down at remnants of broken glassware.

"Umm, that was maybe on me?" Cleo gave me a weak smile. "Who knew that stalking someone on LinkedIn shows you viewed them?"

"Literally everyone," I said as Hugh also said, "Everyone."

Cleo frowned and kept talking. "He called to ask if he could help." Cleo grabbed the trash bag closest to Hugh and tested its weight. I flinched at the sound of broken glass clinking together.

"I came by to change the locks, but he'd already done a lot of damage, I'm sorry Denise," Hugh said.

Sniffing, I gave him a shrug. What could I even say? My heart was aching that someone I knew for so long could be so callous. So vindictive and utterly cruel.

"Hey D, I think I speak for Milk Dud over there when I say, we got you and we got this." She took a long look around the apartment.

"I'll take the family room. Cleo should probably take the bathroom," Hugh said, looking down at the broom in his hands.

Cleo brushed past me and headed towards the back. I grabbed a paper towel off the ground and noticed it was covered in fresh blood. Hugh met my eyes before plucking it from my fingers and throwing it in the trash bag next to him.

"I was hoping I could clean it up before you got back," he said, his tone low.

I attempted a smile, but I knew it was a sad one. His hand cupped my cheek just as Cleo screeched from the bathroom.

"Bitch, I'm glad you packed what you did cuz, girl, that's all you're gonna have!"

I gave a mirthless chuckle and rolled my eyes. Hugh shook his head and dropped a kiss on my forehead before sweeping more glass into the dustpan.

The couch was covered in what had to be several bottles of red wine, and huge slashes across the back through the fabric showed the internal metal frame. Even if I could clean it, there was no way I would be able to salvage it.

The worst, though, was my bookshelf. It looked like he'd tried to tear the metal from the wall and gave up. The LEDs were ripped and hanging. But the books, the ones I'd been keeping safe and secure for decades, were demolished. Some were torn in half, others soaking wet from whatever he'd poured across them.

Throwing off my jacket, I realized I was trembling. I took a controlled breath, closing my eyes to try and slow my heart rate down.

I had two people in my corner here, helping me pick up the pieces. Literally. And there was work to do. Freaking out wouldn't help me. I headed towards the kitchen. Between the three of us, it wouldn't take long to get the place cleaned up.

CHAPTER 11
HUGH

It was past twelve by the time we'd finished a cursory clean of the apartment. But it was still fucked. I'd spent the last half hour wishing I'd done more than make that stupid son of a bitch bleed. The amount of money it was going to cost to replace what he had destroyed was ridiculous.

Cleo may have been joking around in the bathroom, but she wasn't lying. I'd walked around and taken photos before I started cleaning. The tub was full of clothes, covered in food and bleach. Nothing in there was salvageable. I shook my head as Cleo crossed herself, throwing a pair of thousand-dollar shoes into a trash bag.

Anything of value in the place was gone before I'd arrived, and guilt ate at the edges of my conscience. Denise didn't deserve this. This was her place of safety, and no matter how clean we got it or how much shit we replaced, it was never going to feel safe for her again.

Denise stayed silent. She started by cleaning out the fridge, which was dripping in liquid makeup and destroyed makeup palettes. The freezer was full of smashed potted plants. All I heard from her were heavy, sad sighs.

Cleo worked on the living room while Denise moved to the spare bedroom.

Curtis didn't do much damage that I could see but it was a mess from him haphazardly packing up his stuff. From what I could tell, it looked like he'd been sleeping in there. I couldn't imagine having Denise lying next to me every day and choosing to sleep without her.

The girls were on their third trip to the dumpsters. Cleo had handed me a bag to stash for her to take back with her, and I put it off to the side. I was tightening the new knob into place when I heard Cleo talking at Denise.

Denny still hadn't said much of anything, so Cleo and I bickered to drown out the silence. After she'd called me a damn Milk Dud, I'd called her Miss Cleo. It was clearly a sore spot because she'd scrunched up her nose and looked like she wanted to punch me in the face.

Of course, that meant spending the whole night talking with a horrible Jamaican accent and winking whenever she glared daggers at me. Milk Dud became Pudding Cup and then she'd settled on Fudge Pop.

Every so often, we would try to draw Denise into our conversation, but she just looked up at us and gave a fake smile.

"You're staying with me tonight," Cleo said as they walked back through the door.

Denny scrunched up her face and shot her a look of defiance.

Before she could argue, I stood from my crouch in front of the door.

"It's her or me," I said, crossing my arms. Denny's eyes bounced from my bare biceps to my chest, and finally to my eyes. I'd lost the suit jacket and my dress shirt through the night and with the way she was looking at me, it seemed like I was the perfect distraction for her. I was ready to insist on taking her home with me when Cleo spoke.

"Oh, in that case. Den, I am gonna have to take back my offer. I'll be right back with her shit, Fudge Pop." Cleo gave me a smile and winked at Denny before grabbing her coat and the bag of trash I'd hidden, bolting out the door before Denise could even process what had just happened.

Her jaw fell open as she stared at the empty doorway.

I didn't care that she was shocked because she was coming home with me, a place where I could keep her safe. Even if that meant having her in my space, breathing in the scent of her, and knowing that we had a deal that was half done.

"What a fucking traitor," she whispered.

"She speaks," I said, bumping her with my hip.

"Hugh, I'm—"

I cut her off, knowing exactly where she was going. The emptiness in her normally bright eyes was making me ache and I wouldn't be able to handle her trying to minimize this.

"Denise, I swear if you say you're fucking fine..." I narrowed my eyes and watched her sputter.

"I am... thinking—processing." Her hands went to her abdomen, and she breathed into them.

She wasn't as dazed as she'd been earlier, so I resisted the urge to fuss over her. I placed my hands over hers.

"And you can keep doing that. In my guest room. Come back here when you're ready. Or we can help you find a new place. You need to feel safe."

Her eyes went glassy as she blinked back tears. She was looking up at me like I was some puzzle she couldn't make sense of, but she didn't pull away from my touch.

One of her hands turned up to grasp mine.

Her fingers moved across my knuckles and she looked down at my hand, confused. It was clear she was expecting to see scratches or bruises. I'm surprised it took her this long to address the bloody towel she'd seen. I was glad the first thing I'd cleaned up was the piss. Something told me that would've been a bit more shocking.

"You fought." She met my gaze for the first time in hours.

"We did," I confirmed.

"It wasn't your blood." The wheels were turning in her head. If I didn't have a mark on me, the blood came from Curtis. She sat with it for a few more seconds before her lips curved up. Instead of a sad smile, this one was vicious.

"Good," she said it with such conviction that I had to resist kissing the smile off her face and bringing back that lust-filled gaze she'd had for me earlier.

My Little Menace had a dark side. She loved the idea that Curtis had been lying here bruised and bloody, that I'd done that for her.

"If I'd known it would make you smile, I'd have let you get a few punches in too."

She laughed, melodic and light.

That was better. Much better.

I wanted to make her keep laughing and erase this whole shitty day from her memory, but I knew that I couldn't. What I could do was give her a weekend of distraction.

"You're sure?" she asked, hesitant but curious.

She didn't want to be a burden. What she didn't know is if she'd said no, I'd have just stayed outside her complex and made sure Curtis didn't bring his ass back over here.

"Denise."

It was becoming a familiar sparring match. She'd say something ridiculous and I'd say her name, firm, but patient and she'd relent.

"Fine. I'll stay in your *guest* bedroom," she said, as I expected her to. I was fine with that. As much as I wanted her curled up beside me, I wanted her to feel safe, more.

If she stayed here, she'd spend the whole night looking over her shoulder, wondering if Curtis was coming back or what surprise he'd have left for her that she didn't know about yet.

Before I could stop myself, I brought her body into mine for a hug. The warmth of her skin against mine eased some of the pressure that had formed in my chest.

"I've got you," I said.

Her tense shoulders relaxed, and I tightened my hold. This woman.

CHAPTER 12
HUGH

I'd gotten up early to make a plan for the day and to get out some of my rage.

The gym in our building was equipped enough, but what I really wanted to do was box. I hadn't been to my gym in Oakland in months and I hadn't felt the need to. Not until today. I wanted to pummel something. No, I wanted to pummel *someone.*

Leaving Curtis with all of his limbs had been a mistake. If I could go back in time, I'd take his pinkies. It was easy enough to do. I'd spent far too much time perfecting the angle to best sever the tendons, muscle, and bone.

Imagining it filled me with a feral satisfaction that whet my bloodlust. It had been so long since I'd felt bone give way beneath my fingers. Part of me wanted him to come back, wanted him to try me. Unleashing all of this energy on him would be a dream.

That's why I had to get out of the condo early. I couldn't let Denise see that side of me. It's one thing to know that someone exchanged a few blows with someone else, but I knew what I became when Switch took hold. My rage made me feral and ruthless.

It took me years to train it out of my system, to think logically and clearly instead of letting my emotions fuel my decisions. I'd never let Switch into my life, not for anything. At least, I never had before. But there was something about Denise. Watching her, connecting with her. She could tell me to fuck off right now and I would, no questions asked. Hell, she could show up twenty years from today and ask me to help her bury a body and I would take care of it.

She had me.

Watching her quiet and somber last night made me feel helpless and that made me even more angry. I wasn't some twelve-year-old kid anymore and yet... I couldn't fix this. I had to bite my tongue and let Denise feel her feels for the rest of the night. When she looked around the cleaned apartment she wasn't as dejected as she had been.

She only cried once.

Her fingers traced across the edges of a slashed and bleach-stained chair before she looked at the now-empty bookshelf. Something told me he knew just how to hurt her, and her books had something to do with it. By the time we walked out of the apartment, she'd dried her face and was holding a few toiletries that had escaped unscathed.

When Cleo walked up with two full suitcases, Denise didn't even give her a hard time. She just handed her one of the new spare keys and gave her a hug.

When the driver pulled up, I opened her door for her. He came to grab her bags and I turned to look at Cleo.

"Take care of her, Hugh."

I nodded and gave her a hug.

"I will," I replied.

"Don't make me mace you." She winked at me as she turned to walk away.

"Are you sure we can't drop you off?" I asked.

"Nah. I'm four streets up," she replied, already walking up the street with a wave. That didn't stop me from watching her as she walked up the hill and out of sight.

Our ride back to my place was silent. I let it stay that way. I figured Denise needed the space to breathe and think. I'd expected a quip about my ostentatious condo as we pulled up but she barely even looked up as we walked through the lobby and onto the elevators. When we came in I pointed her to the spare room and all she'd uttered was, "Thank you," before she walked inside and shut the door behind her.

I'd stayed up a little late, just in case she came out and needed something, but at two a.m. I called it a night. I didn't need a lot of sleep as it was, but what little rest I did get was haunted by memories of the past.

Switch's memories.

Every time I closed my eyes, I heard the snick of it. His switchblade.

I'd fucked up.

I put in so much work to put all the shit behind me and when I'd seen Curtis I cracked the door and let a little bit of Switch seep in. Now all I could think about was breaking that piece of shit's ribs. And his jaw.

The gym helped. I was able to exhaust myself, sweat through my shirt, and think of anything and everything that didn't include an angry twelve-year-old doing shit that would make grown men puke.

When I walked back inside the house at seven a.m., there she was.

Denise was standing in my kitchen, wearing a tight-ass pair of jeans, that hugged every inch of her delectable ass and a t-shirt that did nothing to hide those gorgeous tits that I immediately wanted in my mouth.

I don't know what I expected when I came back, but it wasn't a fully dressed woman scribbling on a piece of paper. Her face was scrunched up in a look of concentration that was so cute I had to fight every urge not to pluck the lip from between her teeth and occupy her mouth with... something else.

Fuck, I wasn't going to survive this weekend.

CHAPTER 13
DENISE

"Hi?" Hugh shut the front door behind him, a water bottle and towel were dangling from his hand. And he was... very sweaty.

It was mid-morning and I'd slept like a dead person and somehow still woke up exhausted. Part of me was grateful that the shitshow happened on a Friday because it gave me two days to get my game face on before work.

The question in Hugh's voice wasn't surprising. I was also shocked that I was up and facing the day already. But, I didn't have much of a choice.

I could be a puddle, watching sappy movies and second-guessing everything that had happened in my life over the past decade. But, why?

That wouldn't help me fix a damn thing. And if there was something I was good at, it was fixing. So, I got up and got dressed because I was the only person who could fix this.

While sitting in front of the coffee maker, I had already created a running list of everything I needed to do to get things together.

I'd been to Hugh's apartment exactly once and it was the fanciest, most over-the-top condo I'd ever been in.

When he first moved in, he had a housewarming party for a few folks from the office. It was just as remarkable as it had been the first time I'd seen it.

Most people in the city salivated over photos of this fancy-ass place. The complex sat in the very north end of Mission. It was so close to work, I could see our office from his living room window. We were thirty-something stories up and it had all the things a girl could dream of, including a terrace, an infinity pool, and a fancy doorman that knew his name.

I padded back across the kitchen and handed him the untouched coffee.

"Hi," I said.

"I didn't think you'd be up." He took a sip, and I watched his glistening throat move as he drank.

The shirt was so soaked it clung to him, outlining every curve and plane of his chest. Did he always work out that hard? Should I expect this view tomorrow too? Hmm. I turned away so that I wouldn't stare and busied myself making another cup of coffee since I'd just handed mine to the dripping man behind me.

Now that he was back, I tried to school my expression as I ran my fingers along the incredible marble counters in front of me. What I really wanted to do was run around the place like Belle in *Beauty and the Beast*, but I had a feeling he would frown upon me snooping through his personal space. Before the day was up, I definitely was going to spend at least an hour on his terrace, though.

But, before I could reward myself, I needed to get to work on my list. I popped a capsule into the coffee maker and tapped it to start another brew.

"I have a ton of stuff to get done," I said, touching pen to paper.

Hugh frowned and put his stuff down on the island that somehow doubled as a fancy glass cooktop. I could really just live in this kitchen. I wondered how fast the eyes heated up.

"What about processing?" His words were soft, and I took a step back, shaking my head. He wasn't going to convince me to mope. Nope, nope, and no.

"Denny."

"Don't Denny me. Look, I'm fine. See?" I twirled in my jeans, sneakers, and t-shirt. I turned back to the coffee machine to avoid his gaze.

"I'm dressed. I have a list. I'll be out of here tonight. Probably? Maybe... I have to see if they can deliver a new bed in a few hours. I mean, the old one looked fine, but can I really trust anything in there? And the couch, I mean, I can live without a couch for a little while."

Hugh slowly walked towards me as I babbled, his hands came on either side of me and cocooned me in his damp warmth and I shuddered.

"I figure I'll clean-slate the whole thing. And the locks are changed, so that's good. I can get someone to throw everything out and I'll just start over."

He breathed in, inhaling the scent of me, and I bit my lip, partially because I really was babbling and partially because I really loved the feeling of being near this man. My brain went blank as my body became hyper-aware of his touch.

Hugh's fingers slowly stroked the skin on my arm. I sighed. Before I could stop him, he grabbed the list from the counter.

I turned around and made an irritated noise and he just leaned forward, erasing the rest of the distance between us.

"One, you are staying here for as long as it takes. We both know no one delivers furniture in the city in hours. Two, I'm confiscating your list. Having a clean slate is more than just stuff, it's breaking patterns. That leads me to three, you're spending the weekend out. With me."

I looked up at him and gave him a coy smile, leaning towards his mouth before diving right to snatch at my list. Somehow, Hugh saw it coming and held it up, far beyond what I could reach. That didn't stop my pathetic jump for it.

Hugh leaned down and grabbed my neck, running his thumb over my pulse.

"Do that again and it'll be a whole different kind of day, Little Menace."

Before I could reply to his threat or the sensations his touch was causing, he took a step back.

"Be ready in thirty," he said as he walked down the hall, taking my list with him.

Jerk.

CHAPTER 14
DENISE

Hugh's idea of distracting me was art. And, let me tell you, it was an amazing time.

We started our day at the San Francisco Museum of Modern Art. Every corner we turned led to something enchanting. Each piece of art held some nuance that I picked up the longer I looked at it. Every room was stark white and pristine, drawing my focus to the piece on display in front of me.

I fell into a pattern of reading each card, staring at the piece, and reading the card again after I'd taken it all in. Each piece was different and exciting, but the ones that really grabbed me were those that used deep colors that pulled me in.

After a few hours, we found ourselves next door at the Museum of the African Diaspora. I thought I was enjoying SFMOMA, but MOAD took my breath away. Everything was welcoming and warm—the art surrounding us felt like home.

The walls were bold and vibrant. Most importantly, the vibes and energy matched the awe-inspiring art that hung there. I was overwhelmed and head over heels in love. I even found myself doubling back in some rooms because I felt like I didn't get enough of a photo collection or a series of portraits.

I spotted a few mannequins covered in gorgeous prints in the next room and I made a beeline for them. The ceremonial skirts were called Kuba cloths, worn for hundreds of years in what was now the Democratic Republic of the Congo. The card said each square took hours to complete, with the entire skirt taking months.

Designs of all kinds were woven into the fabric, checkered in blue and then black, there were stripes and pieces of material embroidered over some areas. Each small section looked like chaos, but when looked at together, the entire skirt sang.

I spent a long time walking around the skirt in circles to fully appreciate the attention to detail that went into every stitch. It was a struggle not to touch it and feel the fabric beneath my fingers. I went back to the plaque beside it and shook my head. I couldn't believe that it wasn't cotton or polyester.

Hugh continued to let me take the lead as we wandered, when I lingered, so did he. A few times I looked over and saw him studying me and not the art. And, he was smiling, always smiling. It was different, it made his face look younger and less burdened. It was amazing to see. I couldn't help but return it.

By the time Hugh dragged me out, the sun was setting, and my stomach was making hilariously loud gurgles.

"I told you we should've stopped for a real lunch." Hugh had obviously heard my embarrassing stomach.

I shook my head. "The extra time was worth it. The photos of those women in Harlem sixty years ago looked like they could've been taken yesterday. And that Rothko was huge and bright. I could've just dived right into it. But the Kuba cloth! Can you believe that was grass? Insane."

Hugh was standing still and watching me. His hands were in his jeans and his biceps peaked from beneath the short sleeves of his tangerine polo shirt. I turned and walked forward, we weren't very far from his condo and there were a few places near there.

"So, what should we do for dinner? I would make a joke, but I'm star—"

Hugh's fingers grabbed mine and pulled me backward. I squeaked before being cocooned in his warmth and feeling his lips meet mine.

The sounds of the street disappeared and the happy invigoration I'd built all day was met with a feeling of serenity. I leaned into it, loving every second. His tongue found mine as his hand dived into my hair, bringing me closer, as he held me tight.

All the other times he'd held me there was always some urgency, like he couldn't stand not touching me for another moment, but this? This wasn't about seduction. It didn't tell me all the things he wanted to do to my body. It was a culmination of the joy we'd built as we wandered, soaking in history and being near each other.

It was almost too much—too perfect. I pulled back so I could take a breath and I saw emotions at war on his face. His eyes searched mine, and I raised my hand to his cheek.

"I've been wanting to do that all day," Hugh said, his arms still tight around me.

"This was... Thank you."

Leaning up, I placed a kiss on his lips, then his cheek, and his nose. Then I went back to his lips as he laughed.

"Let me get you something to eat before distraction sets in," he let his arms fall, but his hand stayed around my waist and pulled me to his side as we continued down the street.

"Me? I think you're the one confusing me for dinner." I said, nudging his shoulder with my head.

"Gorgeous, you're definitely dessert."

CHAPTER 15
HUGH

Denise truly came to life at the museums.

When she saw us turn the corner and saw SFMOMA, she literally skipped forward. Skipped.

I couldn't keep the smile from my face as she wandered through each exhibit, taking in the statutes and the art. I spent most of my time watching her and barely taking in anything other than her. Her face was so expressive. Everything happened there, probably before she even realized she was thinking it. Of everything at SFMOMA, she was most enamored by the abstracts.

It took some doing, but I managed to get her to agree to a small lunch before pointing to MOAD. She melted as she entered, and I could tell this was going to be her new favorite place. The vibrant colors matched her personality to a tee.

She lingered in front of almost everything, taking her time moving between each room and really giving each piece of history her undivided attention. It reminded me of something my Grams had said about seeing someone's soul when they're in their element.

In MOAD I saw Denny's soul, bright and green and full of life. I soaked it in as we wandered around. This woman was a marvel, and there was no way I was going to be able to get through this weekend without touching her and feeling her against me.

She was, of course, oblivious to the fact that my dick was half-hard. I watched her ass bounce in those jeans as she half-danced around the place and I wanted to pull her into the bathroom.

I needed to buy some art. I wanted her to have that look in private, somewhere with a door that locked and a bed I could throw her down on.

When we walked out, I couldn't help but hold her to me and kiss her. My attention was on her, making sure she was having fun. She was so full of joy and light and after yesterday, I knew she needed it. Being the one that gave it to her had me feeling territorial all over again.

We'd stopped at a pizzeria on the way back to my place. She widened her eyes as I ordered enough food to keep us fed for a few days. While we waited, I texted Cleo a quick update, since I hadn't seen Denise pick up her phone in hours. I also shot a text to my Grams, so she knew that I'd be bringing a guest to dinner tomorrow.

At that moment, I realized this hadn't just been for her, it was for me too. I hadn't thought about Switch all day. There was a space she'd cracked open in my heart and she was filling it with the brightest light I'd ever seen.

It was a short walk back to the condo and I was grateful for it because my stomach was growling as we walked. By the time we hit the elevator, I watched Denny pop a bread knot into her mouth. I raised my eyebrows and she did the hoo-hah as she chewed. Her eyes rolled in bliss as the damn thing burned her tongue, but she didn't seem to mind.

"Eat one," she said, chewing.

I gave her a look, but she was already grabbing one from the bag and shoving it into my mouth.

The perfectly salty bread was fucking delicious. I smirked at her. I kept my gaze locked on hers and I let out a sinful moan as I leaned forward, taking the entire piece of bread and her fingers into my mouth, my tongue tracing across them, sucking the buttery salt from them. When let her fingers go, I slowly chewed on the bread, my eyes not leaving hers.

She blushed but didn't look away. I could see her jaw tick to the side. She was probably chewing on her cheek. What would she do if my knee came up between those thick thighs right now? Would I feel the heat of her lips through my jeans? Would she make that sweet same sigh against my mouth as I thrust my tongue into her mouth?

There was so much I wanted to do with her, *to* her. She had no idea how much control she had over me, how many men turned as she walked by. That wasn't what this weekend was about, but I couldn't help the urge building in me to show her. To give her all the things she should've been getting this whole time. I needed her to see that she could have it all.

As the elevator started to slow down, I winked at her, her cheeks a cute shade of pink. Watching her blush was thrilling. It was the proof I needed that she was just as affected by this as I was, that every time I thought about finding my way into her tight heat, it would be wet and ready for me.

I exited first and opened the condo door for her. I watched as she rubbed her thighs together and bit her lip as she walked out of the elevator.

"Down girl," I heard her whisper to herself as she shut the front door, and I worked hard not to laugh. I wanted to find whoever taught her how to whisper and give them a kiss right on the mouth because she was incapable of saying anything under her breath.

I placed the pizzas down on the coffee table, motioning for Denise to take a seat as I headed to grab a few things.

Moving through the kitchen, I pulled out two plates and some napkins while she opened the boxes and placed them across the coffee table. The smell of cheese reminded me that I wasn't just hungry for pussy, I also needed food.

Denise brushed behind me as I headed towards our seats. Her fingers lightly grazed my ass while I walked past her. She was teasing me. I added another mark to her tally as I turned to watch her.

She leaned up and opened cabinet after cabinet. I would've asked her what she was looking for, but the sight of her on her tippy-toes leaning over my counters was far too appetizing. She finally found what she was looking for and she did a little hop that made all of her jiggle.

The glasses clinked together in her hand as she walked over to grab a bottle of scotch off the liquor cart by the TV.

She poured us both a finger of scotch from the most expensive bottle I had, and I didn't even care. Turning, she saw me watching her path, and she gave me this shy smile that made my chest feel warm.

As she walked over to the couch with our drinks, I smiled. I could do teasing and flirting Denise. Her tongue reached out to taste the amber liquid as her gaze stayed fixed on mine.

"This is good," she said, placing my glass in front of me.

I grabbed a slice of pizza to prevent my fingers from tangling in her hair and drawing her to me. The idea of sipping the rare bourbon right from her lips, the potent and unique taste of her mixed with the oak and hints of caramel. I bit my cheek to stop the moan that was on the tip of my tongue.

We had our game. I had to play my part.

She took a seat beside me and popped a pepperoni into her mouth. Sighing in contentment, I felt that same pressure in my chest form. It wasn't just lust and desire, I wanted her to be happy and content. I was willing to do whatever it took, even letting in the old version of myself, to make sure she stayed that way. I just didn't know if she would be okay with that when she found out about my past.

My phone buzzed and I looked down at it. It was Grams. After I'd followed up her question mark text by telling her that Denise would be coming with me tomorrow, she sent a series of hilarious emojis.

"Grams is excited to meet you."

"I'm—huh?" She blinked up at me.

"You know Grams and I do dinner on Sundays."

"See, I'm following that. I just —"

"Did you expect me to leave you behind?" I raised my eyebrows and watched as she sputtered.

It was a trick question. I wanted her to meet my Grams so she would. I knew Denny would love her. There was no point in arguing, I'd just let her brain work it out while I sat silently watching.

I grabbed her thigh after a minute, and she blinked away whatever line of thought she'd been stuck in.

"Well, no. I mean, I didn't—"

"Good. She's excited to meet you." I paused while she stared at me. "I'm excited to meet her too." My voice went up an octave. I bobbed my head up and down with my words. She gasped and kicked at me with her socked foot.

"Obviously, I would love to meet your grandmother," she said, rolling her eyes and taking another sip of whiskey.

I grabbed a slice of pepperoni pizza and put it on her plate.

"Eat," I said.

I waited until she took a bite before I touched mine.

"Good girl," I said, smiling at the way her breath quickened at my words.

The woman was so easy to read, she craved praise as much as she craved punishment and I was more than capable of feeding both of those desires. I watched her eyes grow hungry and pinball around from my face to my arms and finally to my dick and thighs.

We ate in silence for a bit, me relishing her enjoyment of the food. Her, watching my neck and fingers when she thought I wasn't looking.

I flipped on the TV, mindlessly navigating to my watch list and clicking on the show I had hoped to binge this weekend. Her eyes were burning a hole in the side of my head, and I looked over at her. She was mid-bite, sauce dripping past her mouth.

"What?" I asked. I was confused by her confusion.

"I—this is a choice." She giggled and I rolled my eyes. Yes, it was a British period drama, and yes, I watched it religiously. This woman.

"The new season starts in a few weeks." I opened the show's page and it showed that I'd already watched every episode all the way through. Her eyes scanned the TV before returning to mine. She looked at me for a second before dabbing the sauce off her face.

"How do you even have time to watch all of these? You beat me to work every morning and you're always there when I leave." There was a bit of awe in her tone.

"I don't sleep well. Watching TV helps." I shrugged, answering honestly and crossing my leg over my thigh to get comfortable.

"Interesting. So. The Duke?" She was giving me a look like it was a test.

"Trash." My answer was immediate and honest. That guy was a dick. Sure, he got himself together by the end of the second season, but that woman didn't deserve him putting her through all of that. Denise smiled and nodded.

"That's the right answer. Are we starting from the beginning?" She leaned back and crossed her feet in front of her, sitting her plate on her lap.

"Of course." I clicked episode one and pressed another button on the remote that dimmed the lights. As the episode began to play, I felt her leaning into me.

I could get used to this.

CHAPTER 16
DENISE

We were four episodes deep when Hugh's arm unfolded behind my head, close enough that I could feel the heat of his skin.

A part of me wanted to get up and grab another drink, but I was having too much fun. I'd spent the last few hours slightly grazing his thigh with mine, stretching and feeling the edges of my fingertips dancing along his chest and beard.

I was glad I'd already seen this show, I'd stopped paying attention the moment he moved a bit closer to me. This game was torture. Crossing my legs, I flexed my thighs a bit, enjoying the pressure. I looked down at my foot, an inch from his calf, and absently started to move it left and right.

Hugh stiffened but didn't say a word. We'd made it another five minutes before he stood abruptly and started picking up our plates and leftovers, taking them into the kitchen.

"I think it's time I head to bed," he was avoiding eye contact as he shoved things haphazardly into the fridge.

There were still a few things left on the coffee table. I grabbed them and the empty glasses and padded towards the kitchen. I was turning off the TV when I was pulled backward into a warm embrace.

"Tell me no now, Denny," he whispered into my ear. His length was pressed against the curve of my ass, and I gasped.

"Too bad, I'm tired," I said, even though I didn't believe the words as they came out of my mouth. I squirmed against him as he squeezed my waist.

His hand cupped my pussy through my jeans, and I moaned against the delicious pressure.

"We already talked about lying bad girls." A sharp smack to my thigh made my skin sting and heat. I jerked my body into him, feeling his dick jump behind me.

Lips began tracing across my skin as his fingers grabbed at my shirt, pulling it up and untucking it from my jeans. His tongue found its way up to my earlobe as his hands smoothed along my stomach, his fingers tracing the path of my stretch marks.

"I can wake you up," he said.

Pulling down my zipper, he unbuttoned my jeans. His hand dove beneath my panties as he ran his fingers down the front of my thighs. His grip was tight as his fingertips dragged along my skin and stoked the heat building in me.

My body was alive under his touch. We'd spent so long playing the game, I was practically coming undone in his arms. I'd missed being close to him, feeling myself get lost in desire and passion.

I whimpered as his wet kisses became bites. My jeans were pulled down and before I could come up with something snarky to say. He bit and sucked at my neck. I leaned forward as the pleasure and pain stole my breath.

Hugh let me fall forward and pulled my shirt over my head as I reached for the back of his couch. His lips traced my back as he held tight to my love handles. He was leaving a wet, fiery trail down my back.

I closed my eyes, I wanted to focus on the feeling of him on my skin. My hands covered his around my waist. I was flushing with arousal, simultaneously floating and on fire.

Somehow, I managed to say, "It's past my bedtime."

One of his hands moved and I felt the sting of it hit my ass, coming down hard on my skin. I groaned, biting my hand.

"Before you go to bed, I think I told you I was keeping count. Do you want to guess how many I owe you?" His fingers smoothed over the hot skin of the cheek he'd just reddened. The coarse hair from his beard moved along my back, and I arched, reaching back for him. My fingers finding the warmth of his skin and my heart stuttered.

"Let's play a game. Guess the number without going over, and you'll get a reprieve." Both of his hands were holding my ass still and I wiggled against him.

"Guess too high, you get all of them. Guess too low, you get twice as much."

"That doesn't sound like a fun game," I grumbled against the couch feeling each open kiss move lower.

"Oh, it's fun for me. Because I was keeping track, Little Menace." A shiver ran beneath my skin, and I tried to stand, but between the jeans tight around my thighs and Hugh's hands holding me, I was at his mercy. He felt my struggle and his hands started to slowly massage my skin.

"Remind me: what are your safe words?"

It'd been weeks since I'd said either word aloud. They bounced around in my head every time he caught my eye, and I could see the devilish thoughts playing in his head. I didn't doubt for a second that he would've come up with any and every reason to spank my ass raw. Lucky for him, I enjoyed pushing his buttons.

"Grapefruit for slow, habanero for stop," I said as I felt one of his fingers trace the edge of my thong before pausing, his fingertip gently tapping against my puckered hole.

I held my breath.

"Pick a number, naughty girl."

Something flared to life in my chest, and I fisted my hands into the edge of the sofa, trying to gain a little bit more courage.

"No."

Lips hit the spot between my shoulder blades.

"I think I misheard you," he said, his tongue darting out to lick my back as his fingers moved across my skin, gliding across my muscles. It was an out. He was giving me a chance to be a good girl.

But I didn't want to be good. I wanted to be very, very bad.

"If you're going to punish me, do it." My teeth worried my lip, squeezing my eyes shut. When the pain didn't come, I froze. A full minute had to have ticked by with me, ass up on the couch, and Hugh holding me snug against his clothed waist.

A finger slid into my pussy.

I mewled, trying to move against it, but his hand threaded into my hair and forced my cheek into the couch.

"And we had such a good day," Hugh said, laughing. It wasn't his usual warm-throated chuckle. It was laced with something savage, and I felt my heart flutter because I knew his darkness was what I needed, what I craved.

He moved his finger around and I moaned.

"Such a gorgeous pussy for such a disobedient Little Menace."

His finger dove deeper, and I groaned as he stroked inside of me, slowly and carefully.

"So wet. And responsive."

He pulled his finger free, and I tried and failed to chase it.

I heard lips smacking and he moaned.

"And the taste. That taste is fucking delicious. But that won't save you, beautiful."

His grip on my hair tightened as his thumb entered me. It pumped in and out before another finger replaced it. My legs shook as I tried to lean back until his thumb found its way to my ass.

I froze as he used the wet digit to push down into my tight hole. The burning stretch of my muscles caused me to cry out, but that pain gave way to ecstasy as he stroked the delicate walls of my ass, slow and steady.

His thumb pushed in further, stroking and stretching as his fingers moved out of my hair and around my throat.

"Don't be good now. I thought you wanted to break the rules?" His teeth found their way to my earlobe and bit down.

I growled.

It was like something snapped.

A feral energy wanted to fight back, wanted to be tamed and consumed. Through the haze of lust, I moved my elbow into his side. He oofed behind me. When I tried to turn around, his grip on my throat tightened and another finger joined the one already in my pussy. I clenched down and moved back, finally able to feel the friction I needed.

Moaning, I gripped his hand on my throat, tightening his fingers while I pushed off the couch to fuck myself with his fingers.

I almost came when his fingers clenched tighter on my throat. My moans were gruff and low, nothing like I'd ever heard from myself before.

I was on the edge ready to cum all over his fingers when they were taken away.

My face was pressed back against the couch as a swift slap stung against my ass.

"No, please—"

Two more slaps followed on the same cheek. I wiggled and fought to break away, but it didn't help.

I was at Hugh's mercy.

The spanking was merciless. Each strike was hard and swift. I couldn't tell where the next one was going to come from. Tears came to my eyes as I shouted out over and over. My pussy was so wet that I could feel drips of liquid falling from between my lips.

Then, everything changed.

The pain enveloped me, but so had peace. I took each strike and welcomed it. Every smack against my skin lifted me up and out of my head, and there was nothing to think about, nothing to feel, but the exquisite burning of my beaten skin.

It wasn't about pain anymore, it was about transcendence. Each blow added to the euphoria, and I surrendered to it. I relished in it.

"There she is. There's my good girl." He pulled my hair, and I leaned back, sighing against the sting at my scalp. Fingers massaged my sensitive skin and I shuddered.

He was looking at me with so much admiration. I felt a lump of emotion forming in my throat.

CHAPTER 17
DENISE

His hand was still gripping tight to my hair so we could maintain eye contact. I bit my lip, my mind hazy and high on endorphins and adrenaline. His belt clinked and rustled as I heard him undo his zipper. A hum buzzed around my throat, thinking of what was going to come next.

Letting my hair go, his hands grabbed at my waist as he moved into me, barely. Only the very tip of him was stretching me and I put my face back into the couch, trying and failing to move my hips beneath him. The sounds coming from my throat were guttural, but he stayed still, waiting.

"Hugh," I was pleading and pushing against him.

"Come on Little Menace, you know what you have to do," he said, one hand moving sensually over my skin, his other gripping me at the nape of my neck, holding me down.

"Please," I whispered. "Please, fuck me."

He chuckled as he slowly drew out and back in. I groaned at his slow torture while he laughed.

"Hugh, I need you to—please. More." I fisted the couch as I tried to back into him again, but his grip was unrelenting. I was delirious from the heady mix of pleasure and pain. I needed him.

"Look at how well you beg me," he said, his tone full of reverence. Pulling back, he surged forward, knocking my knees into the couch, and hitting all of the right spots as he planted himself deep inside me.

Humming, I felt my body shaking as he slowly withdrew. I wanted and needed him to fuck me. He slid forward slowly again, this time his thumb had found a home again in my ass, pulling against my tight muscles.

"Do you want me to fuck you here?" He punctuated his words by hooking his thumb and pulling up. I moaned and clenched around him.

He let out a moan of his own in response. I couldn't lean back, but I could—I clenched again and Hugh made a sound in the back of his throat.

The hand in my hair pulled me back and I laughed when I saw the concentration on his face, concentration that creased his forehead and caused him to frown.

Grabbing the back of his neck, I kissed him. It was meant to be a peck, but the heat and tension between us transformed it. Tongues collided as I pulled him to me and whimpered as his teeth bit down on my bottom lip.

I arched my back, pushing against him while his tongue curled against mine.

It wasn't enough. I reached up, pushing hard at his chest. He took a step back and I turned around to face him.

I grabbed his length, slick with my juices, and pulled him forward, finding his mouth again.

Building a rhythm, I moved my hand up and down him. He moaned into my mouth, gripping my hand tightly around his dick, slowing my pace and pushing me backward. As my thighs hit the edge of the couch, he used his free hand to grip my waist and he pushed into me with just the tip again.

I made a frustrated noise as I reached down to grab him, to try and pull him to where I needed him.

His mouth pulled away from mine as his head fell forward. Tangling my fingers in his beard, I dragged his mouth back to mine, tightening my pussy around him. A hand came up around my throat.

"You're going to take all of me," Hugh said, holding everything I desired, just out of my reach.

"And when you get every inch, you're going to say thank you. Aren't you?" He whispered the words against my lips.

I nodded and his fingers squeezed.

"Yes." The word was breathy as it left my lips.

"That's what I thought."

Hugh leaned down, and spit on his dick, using my fingers to rub it around himself before leaning towards me.

"Open."

I opened my mouth and he shoved my fingers inside. I barely processed the sweet taste of my pussy before he lunged forward, roughly impaling me with his dick. His hand moved back to the space between my shoulder and throat while the other was clenched tightly at my waist. My hands clung to his hips as his momentum shoved me back on the arm of the couch. My sore ass twinged but I didn't show it. I was grateful he was finally filling me.

"Thank you. Thank you. Thank you." The moaned words tumbled from my lips as I stretched around him.

Pulling his hips back, he almost freed himself from my grip before he slammed home again.

"That's a good fucking girl. Take this fucking dick, gorgeous."

Everything was on fire as the wide head of his dick danced across my sensitive muscles and hit every sweet spot as he surged forward at a slow and measured pace. I was chasing his every caress, and it only took two more thrusts before I was coming. My orgasm matched his languid tempo. The fingers at my hip grabbed a nipple and pulled it tight. I groaned against the stinging ecstasy as my orgasm lingered.

Sweat was beading along his forehead as he watched his dick work in and out of me.

I grabbed the hand near my throat and reached forward to grab Hugh's cheek. When he looked up at me, I smiled.

"Sir, please fuck me."

Hugh froze. I watched his eyes widen a fraction as he gasped. Angling my face up, I dragged my tongue across his lips and up his cheek.

He leaned into me, and I fell back on to the couch, my pussy still at the perfect angle on his shaft.

"Hold on," he said, grabbing my hips.

I looked around the couch, "To what?"

"Your sanity."

Before I could reply, he thrust into me, bouncing my body against his. I cried out as he pounded into me. My body rocked with each brutal thrust. I couldn't think, I couldn't breathe. The only thing I could do was take him and feel him, my body begging for more.

"Fuck, yes." The words were almost a scream.

Hugh's groans morphed from sensual to feral as he brought me to another orgasm. I moaned through it as his fingers began rapidly rubbing against my clit.

Then, I did scream, my fingers digging into the cushions as I arched into his touch.

"Keep cumming," he groaned.

The dim lights above me blurred as tears fell down my face and my orgasm became so aggressive, that I felt pain in my chest as I struggled to breathe, the tears coming faster.

"Denny, baby?" His fingers stopped moving, but I dug my feet into the couch and kept up with his thrusts.

"Don't you fucking stop," my voice bordered on hysterical.

He grabbed at my hips and kept driving into me, and I wept, repeating my words, begging and pleading with him. Telling him how good he felt and how I wanted all of him. It didn't take long before he found that same unrelenting rhythm and I was coming again, feeling waves and waves of pleasure flowing through my entire body and stealing what little breath I had.

This time, Hugh followed shortly after me, his own orgasm a groaning moan that I wanted to record and keep with me forever. He pumped me full, and I could feel him spasming as he came.

He fell forward as I took heaving breaths in his arms, my body so overcome with sensation it didn't know what to do or how to react.

I felt my body shaking. Hugh crawled behind me, his arms holding me close to him.

My tears kept coming and I couldn't get them to stop. It was like I'd opened some bottomless drawer in myself.

I had no choice but to let everything out before I could close it again. I wasn't sad... I felt free.

His embrace was warm and strong, and I leaned into him, both of us catching our breath and taking in what passed between us. That wasn't sex. Well, not any sex I'd ever had before.

"Hugh?" My voice was hoarse.

"Hmm?" He kissed my shoulder and I smiled at the gesture. This man really was becoming one of the most complex people I'd ever met.

"This was..." I sniffled, there was a lot that I wanted to say, but I couldn't put it into words.

"I know," was all he said.

CHAPTER 18
HUGH

Denise was glued to my front, and we were lying across the back of the couch we'd just defiled. I was folded up like a pretzel and my legs were starting to go numb. I didn't mind because she was in my arms, sweat clinging to her skin, her voice hoarse from pleading with me for every stroke I gave her of my dick.

We were thoroughly spent. My fingers drew patterns against her damp skin as she caught her breath.

When I'd asked her about her punishment, I realized that she yearned for it. She wasn't ready to beg for it... But she would be soon enough.

I don't even think she realized what pain did for her.

It possessed her, released her from all of her frustration to make way for all of that bliss and ecstasy that her mind wouldn't let her feel. For Denise, pain elevated her body from her mind. Her thoughts were stuck on the world outside this room, but when she was occupied with pain, the only thing she felt was hunger for more. For me.

Every stinging slap from my palm worked to bring her to a place where all she felt was euphoria. The tears were a physical release of all the things she was holding tightly coiled inside her.

We sat there for a while longer.

"Okay, I think it's really time for bed."

She stood. Her jeans were locked around her ankles, leaving her gloriously naked from the waist down. She shook her legs free and stretched, her thighs wet as her full lips dripped with our cum. She flinched a little, half reaching for her pussy before she stopped. A hum grew in my chest at the sight.

"I was waiting for you to ask." I stood, watching her bare ass as it bounced. She looked back at her cheeks to see a smattering of bruises already growing beneath the skin. Tentatively, she reached out and brushed one cheek. She didn't wince in pain, but she would feel them tomorrow.

I grabbed her questing hand. My fingers interlaced with hers as we walked out of the living room. When she tried to pull free of my hand to go to the guest room, my grip turned to steel.

"Where do you think you're going?" Displeasure coated my words.

"Pajamas?" she asked. I could hear the annoyance in her words.

"Nah," I replied, dragging her toward my room.

"What do you mean, *nah*?" She couldn't keep the irritation out of her voice and I smiled.

I pulled her in and backed her against the hall closet, watching her breath catch and her eyes go wide. My fingers found her chin and I raised her face up so she could look me dead in the eye.

"When you're riding my face later, I don't want to have to tear anything away from that pretty pussy. You think you're sore now, gorgeous? Just wait."

I pressed a chaste kiss to her lips as she sputtered. There was a look of horror that crossed her face, but I ignored it.

Women will gag on a fat dick, but you ask them to turn your face into a fuck toy and they act like having pussy in the face is an inconvenience.

If I was given a choice, suffocating in Denny's gushing pussy sounded like the way to fucking go.

She enjoyed having my tongue inside her and tonight she was taking a fucking seat, I didn't care if that meant tying her to my headboard. The image of that brought a smile to my lips. Not tonight. But soon.

As we walked into my bedroom, she looked over towards the bathroom and tugged against my hold.

"Am I allowed to pee?"

I scoffed, but let her hand go, watching her move through the open door to the en-suite. I wanted her to go to sleep, full of me, but that just meant I had to cum deep in her later to make up for what she was going to waste now.

It wasn't in my nature to fuck raw. I'd never done it before, no matter how strong the temptation was. Something about Denny made me want to stop being so careful, so methodical, and so planned.

It felt transcendent sliding into her soaking wet pussy with nothing between us. I also knew if she did end up pregnant, she'd make a perfect mother.

But those weren't the reasons I kept emptying deep into her.

I did it because of the look in her eyes, the way she walked around afterward like she didn't know what to do with herself. No other man had cum inside her, made her dripping wet and gushing.

And no other man would.

CHAPTER 19
DENISE

I went through the open door to his en-suite and relieved myself. I flinched a bit as I cleaned myself up, but the soreness was invigorating. As I washed my hands and rinsed out my mouth, I tried to process what had just happened.

The place I'd gone to, the serenity I felt as pain blended with pleasure, calmed my mind. I'd never experienced anything like it before. Normally, I'd be thinking, my brain running with a million and one thoughts, but every time something entered my mind, the Zen I was feeling washed away.

For the first time in weeks, years even, my mind was quiet.

It was such a bizarre feeling, but I liked it. I wanted to feel like this all the time. Is this what I could expect if Hugh and I kept this up?

I wanted this.

I wanted Hugh.

Not just the sex, but the companionship and trust. He gave me something I hadn't had in a long time: a confidant. Even before my life imploded, he was there. And I just never realized how much I needed and appreciated that until now.

Hugh was standing there, looking at his phone when I came back in.

The last twenty-four hours proved that he was more than just someone I could trust, he was someone I could fall in love with.

Whoa there, brain, *whoa there*. Skirrrt. Skippity-boo-bap. First, I was thinking about what ring he'd buy me and now I was talking about love? I knew I was zenned out, but that was too much. I mean, I love Hugh. My friend, Hugh. But *love* love? I blew out a breath. I clearly needed more orgasms to smack some sense into me because...

"Come here." He held out his hand.

Without hesitation, I walked forward and took it.

"I'm gonna make good on that promise, but I'll let you get in a little nap."

Good. Good.

This I could do. Shit-talking, flirting, and a little side eye.

I scoffed, "I think you need a nap just as much as me, old man. Might want to pee, I'd hate for you to have to wake up--"

He pushed me down to the mattress while he threw his phone down and stripped.

"I used the bathroom in the hall." He pulled his shirt over his head. I'd never get tired of looking at this man naked. The tattoo on his arm looked even more menacing in the shadowy room. It curled up from his wrist to his shoulder. The shapes moved and swayed with each other. He was strong, but he didn't have a six-pack. His body was thick and muscular, I watched as his biceps bunched as he yanked off his pants and briefs.

"And, I'll always find the energy for you."

I blinked at him. What were we talking about again?

"Take that bra off, Denise." That familiar niggle in the back of my brain whispered to me, reminding me that I didn't *have* to do shit. As fun as she was making this, my bad girl tank was tapped out and I didn't have it in me to push back.

I flipped the hooks behind my back and slid the cups off.

"You're always so bossy," I said, throwing the bra at him.

He caught the strap and placed it on his dresser as I threw back the covers and laid down.

"You love it when I'm cocky," he said, leaping over me to the center of the bed. He held me tight, his warm skin heating mine as we tangled our feet. I could feel his heart beating against my cheek. I smiled. It had been so long since I'd laid next to a naked man. Had I always fit into them like this?

"It's because you know how to use it," I whispered, yawning. I grabbed the cover, throwing it over us both.

"Damn right, I do." He snorted and I pushed against his chest as he rubbed his beard against my face.

"I like your tattoo," I said, feeling his hand in my hair.

"Thanks, I designed it myself."

"What is it?" I asked, rubbing at my eyes.

"Switch." Before I could ask him what he meant, he started to rub my back, slowly touching my skin with the pads of his fingers. I started to drift away.

I could get used to this.

CHAPTER 20
DENISE

I was dragged awake by a tongue drawing circles against my shoulder. When I pried my eyes open, I saw it was still dark and groaned. I didn't know what time it was but I knew it was sleep time. The wet warmth of his tongue was insistent and gentle. I sighed against it before I said his name.

"Hugh."

"Hmm?" His hand on my stomach started to explore, his caresses leaving tingles across my skin and a familiar heaviness between my thighs.

He knew exactly why I'd called his name. I was still so sleepy.

"Hugh!" I cried out as his teeth replaced his tongue, sinking deep into my flesh as his questing fingers dipped past my stomach, resting just against my pussy.

"Oh, did you want to sleep? I can—" He shifted to move his hand away and I grabbed it to hold it there.

"Well. I mean, you're already there and we're both awake, you might as—"

Two fingers dived into my pussy, and I arched into them as his palm ground against my sensitive clit.

I moaned as he laughed into my shoulder.

"You were such a good girl, I wanted to make sure you got your reward. Do you want your reward, gorgeous?" His tone was so soft, so full of adoration. A host of butterflies took flight in my stomach, and I was surprised I didn't take float off into the stratosphere with them.

There were a lot of things that I wanted to say, but I settled on, "I love rewards."

"Mmm, because you're a good girl. Say it." His lips had climbed up my neck and his words were whispered against my ear.

I felt a blush move into my cheeks as his fingers moved.

"Because I'm a good girl."

His hand came to my neck, and he pulled my lips to his. It was another slow and sweet dance between us. I loved the aggression and heat, but when his lips sipped at mine like he was taking a long taste of me, I melted against him. Our tongues curled together in an unhurried rhythm. He dragged me forward until I was lying on top of him.

I pulled back, my lips moving across his cheek, my tongue darting across his neck and sucking at the skin above his Adam's apple.

"Come sit down." His hands went to my hips, and I moved to straddle his waist. "Not there."

"Umm, I think—" I stuttered the words and was promptly cut off.

"Climb up here and sit down." He was using his grown man voice that would normally make me turn into the world's softest marshmallow. I pushed back from his chest and looked down at him.

"I can lay down."

He gave me an impatient look and jerked my whole body forward until my nipples were swaying in his face.

"Remember one tap for yes, two for no." I shook my head and he nodded.

Hugh's hand traced my cheek, and he gave me a wide smile. "Do you trust me?"

I nodded. He threw the pillow from behind his head to the side as he kept his eyes on mine.

"Grab the headboard. And sit."

My lip went between my teeth as I looked up at the low wooden headboard and back down at him. His hands went to my thighs, and he urged me up.

After another second of indecision, I did as I was told.

Grabbing the headboard, I moved until I was crouching, hovering over his face and putting all of my weight onto my arms. When I stopped moving, he slid his hands up my thighs and pulled me down.

Lips captured my clit and sucked, and I shouted, burying my face in my arm. His tongue lapped at me, and I shuddered against him. I felt a hum rising in my chest as he feasted on me.

"Are you okay?" I asked.

His hand tapped once against my thigh.

I was trying to stay as still as possible, but when his tongue dove into my entrance, I sat back further and tilted my hips, moving against his wet, warm thrusts.

Hugh made a noise of appreciation and encouraged my hips backward and forward as his tongue fucked in and out of me.

"This feels so good," I said, my voice full of surprise. It wasn't just his talented tongue, it was the feeling of control. He was giving me control over him, letting himself be vulnerable as much as I was vulnerable. That was just as intoxicating as the tongue lapping at my clit.

As my orgasm built, my hips went from back and forth to a circle. I used my leverage on the headboard to work my hips. When Hugh's tongue slid out of my pussy, I felt bereft. I tried to shift my hips to chase it, but he held me still and his mouth covered my clit and sucked.

"Oh, don't stop."

My orgasm was sharp and blinding. I sat up, pushing down harder on his face as his tongue continued to lick and suck as my pussy gushed. Each gulp of air, each flick of his tongue pulled another wave of my orgasm forward and I was overcome.

I couldn't think, I couldn't breathe. I was going too high, it was too much. Another orgasm was building right where the other had left off.

"Stop." I moaned, my hips still fucking his face. My hands went to the sides of his head as I moved my hips to chase his tongue.

When his mouth settled back on my clit and his fingers dove into me, I cried out as another orgasm rocked through me. His fingers angled up as his tongue circled and flicked and I was shaking, tears crept from eyes as my whole body tightened above him.

I reached down and felt his throat, the muscles were clenching and moving as he devoured me.

"Fuck, fuck, fuck."

My body was clenching. I was rocking and I couldn't breathe, all I could do was feel. I felt ethereal. This was nirvana. His tongue lapped at my clit as another finger filled me. My hands fell to my nipples, squeezing and twisting, my hips meeting each thrust of his fingers. Every rock of my hips sent electricity through my body.

My orgasm crept up and I went still. Hugh's mouth sealed over my clit again and sucked. My mouth fell open in a silent scream. Liquid gushed, and my lungs seized as they begged for air.

I leaned forward and tried to move away, but Hugh's arms hooked onto my thighs and held me still against his mouth as his tongue continued to assault my pussy. The pleasure was so sharp, so deep, it felt like I was falling apart.

Sobbing moans left my mouth as he kept up his pressure and pulled me harder onto his face. His mouth and tongue were relentless and showed no signs of stopping.

Everything was sensitive, every sweep of his tongue felt like I was being licked by delicious fire. I was out of my mind and being driven my overwhelming pleasure.

I couldn't do it. I couldn't survive another orgasm. I wailed and squirmed, grabbing at the headboard as I said the word.

"Gr-grape-grapefruit. Grapefruit." The words were a whine.

My hips continued to rock against him, but his mouth released its abusive hold on my clit.

He began kissing my pussy lips and my thighs as I shook around his ears.

Hugh's fingers were still deep inside me, and I rocked slowly against them, whimpering, and trying to remember how to fill my lungs with oxygen.

Pulling myself up, I dragged my shaking legs back and my pussy away from his mouth. The way he'd held me to him had me wondering if the man had gills.

I looked down at Hugh's face, my own dripping in sweat, as I leaned against the headboard.

His eyes were full of heat.

Instead of saying I told you so, he licked his lips, savoring the taste of me.

"I need you to fuck me, beautiful."

CHAPTER 21
HUGH

I'd never been so hard in my life. And it was all because of Denise. Just when I thought I knew what to expect, there was another surprise waiting for me.

She was an enigma.

She'd hovered over my face like she was embarrassed, almost apologetic, until I stuck my tongue inside her and lapped at her cream.

That was all it took for her to let go and become the vixen I knew she could be, her thighs tightened around my head while she moved. Her cries of ecstasy filled the room as she writhed above me.

Once she came the first time, she was uninhibited. She took what she wanted from there, hips gyrating as she fucked my face and fingers.

Then, I was the one seeing God.

All I could think of was her, the sounds she was making, the warmth of her skin and the feeling of her muscles rippling as she came over and over again, thrashing against my face.

Making her cum was my way of worshiping her. My benefaction.

Every one of her orgasms was a delicious benediction. And with each one I was more and more sure I wanted to praise this woman for the rest of my life. Lie prostrate on her altar.

She was still clutching the headboard, her face resting against it as her chest rose and fell and her body shook. My face was dripping in her sweet juices. I would've drowned in them if she'd let me.

"I need you to fuck me, beautiful," I said.

I couldn't be trusted, if I flipped her over and drove myself into her right now, I would be rough. And she didn't need rough, not now.

She pulled her hips back and reached toward my weeping dick. I bit my tongue to stop the hiss from leaving my mouth. Jesus, one touch from her, and I was ready to shoot all of my cum onto her pretty hands. I stilled the fingers stuffed inside her.

Slowly, she fisted me, her fingers slipping up and down along my shaft. Before I could beg her to put me out of my misery, she brought her hand to her mouth and licked her palm, her tongue swirling as she moaned against it, cleaning it.

Fuck.

This woman was mine. No other man would ever get to see this sight, feel the warmth of her skin, the feeling of her soft and wet heat.

Her pussy was hovering near my chest as she leaned back to continue her torture, but I couldn't take it anymore. I bit at her thigh and pulled my fingers free from her. She cried out at the loss of them. I smacked her clit and watched her yelp as she shuffled back a little more.

"Make yourself cum on my dick."

Her tits swung in my face, tempting me with a taste, so I took a bite.

She yelped, smacking my chest. I chuckled as her lips trailed across my neck and she bit me back.

"They were right there, Denny. I'm only a man," I groaned the words as she pulled at my skin with her teeth and started to kiss her way down my chest.

I could practically feel her roll her eyes as she began to tongue my skin. She was torturing me. Each movement was slow and calculated. Her fingernails dragging across my skin, her tongue darting out every so often to lick as well as kiss.

I let her take control even though I was yearning to dig my hands into her hair. The desire to make her do what we both wanted was eating at me. I was almost vibrating with the need to make her submit, to sit her tight pussy down and keep making her shake, milking me until I came inside her.

She deserved gentle as much as she deserved rough.

And as much as my balls ached to let loose inside her again, I let her move at her pace. Her pussy grinding on my face didn't kill me, but if being teased to death by this gorgeous goddess was it for me, I'd happily take it. Please, and fucking, thank you.

Denise leaned back, her fingernails dragging up my thighs and past my hips. I groaned, watching her mouth tilt up as she smiled. My dick jumped against her skin as she positioned her hips over mine.

She looked down at me, that same silly glint in her eyes as she licked her lips. Her fingers touched my soaking beard, and I brought my hands to her thighs.

Smirking, she tapped my chest twice with her palm, "Maybe I am tired after all—"

Oh, absolutely not.

I reached up and grabbed her by the waist as I thrust up into her, pumping her full of my dick. I moaned as she gasped, her eyes drifting shut. Her hands flew to my chest as fingers dug into my skin so she could support herself.

I lowered my hips back down to the bed, feeling her muscles caressing and squeezing me as she settled her weight into me. She took a breath, and I watched her lips part as she adjusted to having my dick seated deep inside her.

"Nah. You're gonna fuck this dick. And, in the morning, I'm making waffles."

She blinked once and then twice before bringing both of her hands up to her face as she giggled. The elation in her giggles set me off and I laughed as she rested her forehead against my chest.

I felt my cheeks start to heat. Who in the hell quotes *Shrek* while they're fucking? Especially when they're dick-deep in a pussy that had them wondering if the meaning of life could be found seated between two perfect thighs.

"Hugh," she said, still laughing.

"Denise," I replied.

"Donkey!" she yelled.

That was it. Now we were both cackling, shaking the bed with full-on belly laughs. I felt her pussy clenching as she snorted. She must've felt it too because as she continued to giggle, she tilted her hips and gave me the friction I'd been waiting for.

My laugh turned to a hiss as she leaned back toward my legs and gave me the glorious view of our bodies joined together before she moved her hips. I watched her pussy cling to my dick, hugging it tight as she took her sweet time moving up and down on me.

She bit her lip as she concentrated on her movements. God, this view. I didn't know how long I could hold off on coming.

"I'm really expecting waffles," she moaned.

I reached forward, my fingers moving up and down on her wet slit, teasing her.

She slammed down harder and found a delicious rhythm, bouncing up and down, her tits deliciously swaying just out of reach. I rested my hand on her hip as she tightened on me, she was close to coming and so was I.

"You keep fucking me like this, you'll get more than waffles. Your name will be on my deed. And I'll put *my* ring on that fucking finger."

She shuddered, bouncing faster, sliding up and down on me as I circled her clit. I was teasing her, watching as she worked herself more and more to chase her orgasm. My chest clenched tight at the sight of her riding me and chasing her pleasure.

It was worth the test of my control to watch her body dance above me. But I needed her to cum. I wanted to see the ecstasy etched on her face as her eyes rolled back and her spirit moved outside of her body. I moved my fingers quicker, chasing her as she fucked me.

"It's all yours, Little Menace. Just come all over this dick."

I pinched her clit. She threw her head back as her orgasm rippled through her, her tight pussy bearing down on me as she paused. I bit my lip, watching her mouth fall open.

I couldn't hold back. My patience was gone.

I grabbed both of her hips and thrust up into her, feeling her muscles continuing to tighten down on my dick. She kept moaning and clenching as I felt my own orgasm drawing tight at the base of my spine.

"Fuck. Oh, fuck." I came, stuffing her full of me, as her orgasm clenched me tight. I moaned as I slowed my pace. Fighting against the sensitivity, I pumped in and out of her before I pulled out, chuckling as she made a noise of protest.

She fell to my side, and I leaned forward, grabbing the blankets and cuddling against her. Her whole body was trembling. There's no way she wasn't going to feel this in the morning.

I was making my woman waffles.

Her hand came up to my wet beard and she tugged at it before her breathing evened.

Pulling her tighter, I heard a soft snore and I smiled.

I leaned down to watch her face, softened in sleep. My lips moved to her face, and I gently ran them across her eyelids and lips.

"Right where you belong, gorgeous," I whispered against her lips.

We had a deal and now that deal was complete.

But she didn't say anything about touching and kissing. I was going to keep her as close to me as I could until I was forced to show her who I really was, and I lost the chance to hold her like this again. She was going to be mine until then.

CHAPTER 22
DENISE

Rustling pulled me awake. It was far too bright in the room. I put a pillow over my face and groaned. It didn't matter what time it was, it was entirely too early. Hugh chuckled and threw the blankets off me.

"Fuck off," I mumbled, kicking a leg up at him which I immediately regretted.

My everything was sore.

"Come on, sit up." He grabbed the pillow from my face and threw it to the other side of the bed.

"Let me die here!" The wail was dramatic, but I couldn't truly be expected to leave the bed when even my eyeballs hurt.

Hands gripped my ankles and dragged me backward. I refused to open my eyes or fight, so I went limp.

"I gave you a choice," Hugh said, his tone playful.

Hands circled my waist and knees yanking me forward and...up? I was ready to be dropped on my feet but instead, I was being held. Hugh was carrying me somewhere. I leaned into his neck and his skin was damp like he'd already showered.

His chest was covered in a soft cotton shirt, and I snuggled into it, not a care in the world that I was still butt-ass naked.

This was becoming a very suspicious pattern, me naked and him clothed, and frankly, I didn't mind. Just like I didn't mind clinging to his neck and being whisked away and—oh my God.

This was it.

The moment every romcom lover waits for: Hugh was my Kevin Costner.

I started humming *Queen of the Night* as he carried me into the bathroom.

I peeked and saw that the lights were dim, and it felt muggy. He'd definitely been up for a while. Clearly, he was a morning person. Gross.

Hugh snickered as I started to sing. He held me over his big ass tub and slowly lowered me into the water. I protested immediately as the heat seared my skin.

"Stop, you're fine," he said, plopping me all the way into the water. I sat still for a few seconds as I adjusted to the heat and sighed as my muscles loosened.

"I'll be back, Whitney." He gave me a long look before walking away. I sang the high notes in the chorus to his back and smiled as his laugh boomed around the room.

He'd drawn me a bath. A hot as fuck bath because he knew I'd be sore from all of our... activities last night. I smiled and leaned back in the water, feeling it completely cover me. This tub was a dream. Hell, all of this was a dream.

As annoyed as I was that I was boiling like barbeque short ribs in a crock pot, it gave me time to think and breathe.

In the back of my head, I knew we were in some bubble. In here, we could keep doing this and nothing else would ever have to change.

But, for now, I couldn't think about change. I was embracing the Denny that threw my bitch ass boyfriend in a cab and stepped out of an elevator to get mine. The Denny that gave Curtis the finger when he'd lied to me. The one that was tired of his gaslighting and leeching.

That little voice in the back of my head was chittering at me, reminding me that I'd cheated on Curtis. And I wasn't innocent, not by any means, but I reminded that voice that you can't cheat on something that doesn't exist. And Curtis had stopped being my partner a long time ago and he'd become my dependent.

Hugh didn't need some sugar mama to pay his bills, he was accomplished and loaded, and he wanted me, not financial stability.

Being here with Hugh was never something that I'd considered before. But I'd also never considered Hugh before, I mean, not seriously. My mind would sometimes wander to him, but it was always some scenario that felt far-fetched and impossible. But now that I was here, I couldn't imagine a different outcome. I was putting the pieces together, trying to see what I'd missed.

When did things change for him? Was there always something simmering between us, and I'd just missed it? I'd been oblivious to Curtis, was I just as unaware of Hugh?

I mean, the way he fucked me into oblivion was one thing. But yesterday. That was something... else. The whole day, not just the sex...

Taking a deep breath, I closed my eyes and focused on my senses, not on my racing thoughts. The scent of sage and coconut oil was soothing. The heat from the water was relaxing and the silky feeling of my legs meeting beneath the water was delicious. My face started to heat at the memory of Hugh's hands on me, his thumb teasing my asshole. That was new... And I didn't hate it?

Who the fuck was I becoming? A new me? An unhinged version of myself? I leaned back further as the heat surrounded me. Right now, I was a pampered bitch. All that was missing was —

Footsteps echoed against the tile as Hugh walked in carrying a bellini and a bowl of fruit.

Food and a little drinky drink? Was this man proposing, because yes. I smiled to myself.

"What's that smile?" he asked as he bit his lip, handing me the glass.

I took a sip and nodded, changing the subject, "Thank you, this is nice."

Hugh leaned down, giving me a kiss before popping a grape into my mouth.

"It makes me happy to see you happy, Denise." There was so much warmth in his voice. Who was this man? My smile made my cheeks hurt.

"I *am* happy."

Hugh fed me another grape and a strawberry before excusing himself, adjusting his pants on the way out of the bathroom.

I laughed.

Apparently, a man can only take so much torture before he had to tap out.

After a while, the water started to cool, and I knew it was time to get up. Thoroughly pruned, I grabbed the towel he'd left for me and dried off. I could see the bruises, bright against my ass, and I smiled, tracing the outline of one that was darker than the others.

My muscles still protested as I moved, but they felt much better than before. I spared a glance at the bruises on my arms, the color had begun to fade a bit and I could only see the yellow and green if I looked really hard. The scratches were scabbed over, and I inhaled as I poked at one.

It was so bizarre to compare the two. One was done in anger and the other with affection. Somehow Hugh and I had gone from fucking to indulging in each other and something far more. It took me by surprise.

The man had offered to let me move in. Not just, stay for a few days and get your bearings, he said he'd put my name on his deed.

Now, I'm not a whole fool, I know men say next-level shit when they're balls deep in something good, and once that post-nut clarity hits, they walk it all back and find a way to gaslight you into believing that they never said that.

But that wasn't Hugh. Sure, I hadn't been fucking him for very long, but we'd been friends for years. Had I been oblivious to how he felt the whole time? I stared at my unruly reflection and pulled at my hair. It wouldn't be the first time that I was blind to a man.

Finding mouthwash, I gave it a little swirl and cleaned my face.

I wasn't blind to this man now, not anymore. And, while we were still in this bubble, I was going to do everything I could to take advantage, like fucking him, hopefully on top of his expensive marble counters. A pleasant soreness was still lingering between my thighs.

There was no way I was doing any of the work, but a girl has needs.

There was a robe hanging behind his bathroom door. I wrapped it around me, surprised that it fit. I wondered what else in his closet would fit me as I walked into the bedroom and took a look at my phone.

I had several missed texts from Cleo last night and this morning, each one more explicit than the next.

Hey boo, how are you feeling?

Are you getting your back blown out? You are, aren't you? Yes, BITCH!

Is it good? I hope it's good. You deserve to drown in that man's big ass dick.

Come on, tell meee!

Don't tell me. I'm jealous and horny, and I may kill you and wear your skin like a suit.

If you're reading this, you should be gargling, fucking, and sucking.

Slurp slurp, gobble gobble, glug glug.

Hovering over the keys for a minute, I replied.

Yes, I'm fine. And yes to everything else. I'll update you later, love you.

I put the phone face down and walked out toward what smelled suspiciously like pancakes.

True to his word, the bar had two plates of Belgian waffles with another bowl of fruit waiting. I expected to see a mess, but the kitchen was just as pristine as it was last night.

"Are you a witch? Wait, is there some Brakebills shit going on in here?"

"Some... what?" He looked confused.

I clapped giddily.

"Okay, first, this looks amazing. Thank you. I'm very excited that you were serious about waffles because—yum. But, I also get to watch you watch *The Magicians* and that's going to be—amazing."

Leaning up, I brushed my lips against his, only for him to pull me closer and tease my mouth open, giving me a very slow and deliciously thorough kiss.

"Good morning," he whispered the words against my lips.

I sighed as my butterflies fluttered hard against my ribcage. I half-expected them to go full-Alien out of my chest. "Good morning," I whispered back. My hand that had found his chest began to move, dipping lower until he stopped me.

"Breakfast," he muttered, kissing my cheek.

"Or?" I grabbed his hand to pull it under the robe.

Hugh's gaze darkened and he captured my mouth again, pushing me backward while his fingers tightened on my nipple. I moaned into his mouth as his fingers caressed my chest and grabbed at the edges of my robe.

Instead of tossing it open, he pulled it shut and belted it tight before pushing me one more step back and making my butt hit the chair at the bar. He turned me to face the counter, and I groaned.

"We had a deal. Eat." He patted my head like I was a toddler and gave me a wink while taking a seat beside me and picking up his own fork. Deal? A waffle deal? To my horror, I felt my lip pout.

"But—" A mouthful of syrupy goodness was shoved in my mouth, and I moaned as I chewed. Crunchy and soft, chewy, and not too sweet.

"Holy. Shit." I picked up my own fork and dived in. If he didn't magic these up, I needed to know where the fuck they came from and how I could have one in my face every single day for the rest of my life.

I was reaching for a raspberry when I noticed Hugh hadn't touched his food. At all. His eyes were glued to my mouth. I licked syrup off my lips and watched as his own tongue traced his lips. I shook my head and waved my fork at him.

"Nah, no take backsies. Eat your waffles and stop eye-fucking me." I furrowed my eyebrow and gave him what I hoped was my, *I'm eating, don't try me* face.

He reluctantly used his fork to stab at his own waffle, adjusting his pants as he grumbled.

CHAPTER 23
HUGH

It didn't take us long to eat breakfast. With the sounds she was making and the way the creamy skin of her throat moved, it was a struggle not to make her my breakfast.

But, I was a man of my word and our two nights were through. I wouldn't fuck her again, even if that meant being tortured by her parading around naked under my robe, smelling like me.

Before she could offer, I got up, and grabbed her plate, using it as an excuse to lean over her and take a deep breath, familiarizing myself with my scent on her skin. I needed to memorize it, to let it soak into my senses and my pores.

She made me unsteady. I kept second-guessing myself.

For the first time in decades, I let Switch out of his cage to have a conversation with her shit-eating ex. My Grams would've had a heart attack if she knew. She'd spent so much time praying for me and pleading with me to get my shit together. The idea of letting her down made my heart literally ache.

Switch was young and reckless. He didn't plan. He wasn't meticulous. And he damn sure couldn't have built this life for himself. Regression back to who I used to be wouldn't help me keep what I had. But, if it helped keep the people I cared about safe, I would play with fire.

I forced those thoughts out of my head and thought about the temptation sitting behind me. It was so easy for me to lose myself in her. Her pussy, the bright and cheery outlook she had on everything around her. How could she be so unblemished by life?

I wasn't expecting her. But now that she was here, I welcomed her. She awoke something in me that I'd fought for so long. She wore down the defenses I'd built, and I don't think I could let her go if she asked me to now.

"I try to get to Grams's by three. There's a game on in a few if you want to watch it?" I leaned against the fridge, trying to put some distance between us. As she sat, the tie around her waist loosened and more and more of her soft skin was peaking, just for me. I wanted to taste her, feel her pulse beating hard against the palm of my hand.

She was smiling at me, oblivious to the turmoil boiling under my skin.

"Can I bring something?" she asked, scooting forward and showing off the soft skin of her thighs.

I had images of her, teasing me while hovering above my aching dick. Her face, contorting in ecstasy as she fucked my face and tightened those thighs around my ears.

"No." The word was a growl and she frowned at me as she shoved me out of the way to look in the fridge.

"Okay, grumpy." She bent over and the robe rose up and showed off the bruises I'd peppered across her ass.

I bit my cheek until copper replaced the memory of her cum on my tongue.

"She's not expecting you to bring anything, Denise," I ground out.

I *was* grumpy and I knew it was unfair to take it out on her. Just the thought of her delectable ass had me dreaming of living balls deep in her and she was literally walking around with her juicy ass hanging out.

I grumbled and turned away from her. Fucking her was transcendent, but if she wanted me, she had to come to me, and we had to make a new deal.

When I was inside her last night, I'd promised her everything. And I meant it. I would give it all to her, all she had to do was ask.

CHAPTER 24
DENISE

"If it ain't my baby!" Hugh's grandmother's husky voice carried clear across the yard and out to the street.

The gate to the front door of a gorgeous Victorian home slammed open the second our ride pulled to a stop. With its tall and narrow windows and gothic style, my mouth fell open in awe. I was immediately obsessed, and I couldn't keep the smile off my face. The house was painted classic white, but the trim was a bold and dark purple. The yard was bright green and neatly trimmed and the planters were full of giant and colorful flowering bushes. I could tell this was a happy and well-cared for home.

We walked up through the yard starting to feel nervous. I'd heard so much about her, I really hoped that she was okay with me crashing on her time with her grandson.

"Grams, I'm here at the same time, every Sunday." He tried to sound annoyed, but it was clear he loved the attention.

She had to be in her seventies, because math, but she didn't look a lick over fifty. Not a hair was out of place as she descended her front steps and squeezed her grandson tight before shoving him out of the way.

"Denise! I have heard so much about you!" She squeezed me just as tight as she did Hugh and ushered me forward. "You can call me Grams too, Sugar. I'm not a fan of all that formal shit. Come on, come in."

I'd somehow managed to keep a tight grip on the container of potato salad I insisted on making earlier. It was the polite thing to do. I never showed up anywhere without bringing at least something with me.

But, I had also wanted to peruse that man's fancy ass kitchen. And peruse I did. For someone who works stupidly long days, he had the most stocked kitchen I had ever seen. Everything was top of the line which made sense because he could apparently cook his ass off.

Even though everything was so clean this morning, he'd made our waffles and left them in his toaster oven until he heard me leave the bathroom. He'd cooked, cleaned, and made sure I ate, all after sending me flying through the fucking cosmos with so many orgasms my pussy was still pulsing angrily twelve hours later.

Hugh had to be some demigod in disguise. Men this perfect and single don't just fall out of the sky.

After telling me at least eight times I didn't need to bring anything, he gave up and sat down to watch the game. I was a little surprised that he didn't do much beyond kissing me good morning, but I was so blissed out and excited by his kitchen, I didn't mind.

After I threw on a pair of jeans and a flowy long sleeve shirt, I was lucky to find, I spent the rest of my time on the terrace, dozing while the potatoes and eggs boiled and cooled.

"So, he finally broke you down, huh?" Grams whispered and I leaned in close.

"Finally?" Hugh had talked to his grandmother about me enough that this was a *finally* moment? I took a breath. Grams laughed and I gave a breathy laugh and slid my gaze to Hugh who was holding the door open for us.

"What's so funny?" He narrowed his eyes at us.

I bit my lip and Grams just shrugged. So, I wasn't the only woman in his life that gave him a hard time? And to think, I thought he had every woman around him wrapped around his finger. This was going to be fun.

She ushered us into the living room and Hugh took my potato salad to the kitchen.

"You wouldn't believe what happened down the street, Hugh." Grams looked like she was bursting to gossip as she yelled from the living room. Hugh came back and sat next to me, his fingers finding mine and giving me a little squeeze.

"Charles—he used to be the butcher back in the day, Denise—came home and realized his power was out! So, he called up the power company, spitting mad and cursing. They asked him to walk out and check his breaker. That wasn't the problem. It was the raccoons!" She paused for dramatic effect. Hugh and I laughed.

"Then he started yelling at Regina—that's his next-door neighbor, Denise—because she's been feeding them damn stray cats for years and apparently that blind bitch can't tell the difference between a cat and a raccoon because a whole family stops by for breakfast, lunch, and dinner."

I imagined an old woman blindly throwing cat food in her backyard and shook my head. Hugh was reclined on the sofa and covering his eyes, his smile wide.

"He was screaming so loud the whole neighborhood came out. And then Patrice, you know Patrice is always stirring the damn pot, she came out with a bowl of popcorn. We shared it as Charles started kicking that poor woman's garden gnomes."

"Not the gnomes, Grams! Those should be declared a landmark." Hugh's tone was full of mirth.

"I hate those damn things," she said to me as she rolled her eyes. "But Hugh, he's always loved them."

"I used to cut her grass back in the day. She said when she passes, she's leaving me those gnomes." Hugh eyed his Grams as her lips thinned to a line.

"I swear, you bring them near my house, and they'll decorate your grave." Her tone was serious, but apparently not serious enough because Hugh started belly laughing.

"Don't worry, Grams. I would *never*."

Even I could hear the bullshit in his tone.

"*Bull. Shit*," she said through her teeth, shaking her head.

Oh. I *liked* her.

CHAPTER 25
HUGH

The women were glowing. It was like I'd touched two live wires together and I was watching the fireworks explode. Dinner was delicious, as always, and Denise was talking recipes with Grams. Denise was saying her secret to a good roast was balsamic vinaigrette, and Grams was swearing by a healthy coat of mustard.

I should've known those two were going to spend the day testing my patience right then and there, but I didn't think that far ahead, I was just excited to introduce them to one another.

Grams had her gray hair curled around her ears and I was watching her, curious. There were two reasons why she would look this good: she was trying to impress Denise, or she was going over to see Mr. Parker.

As much as I loved the idea that she'd dressed up for Denny, I knew it was Mr. Parker. They'd been *friends* for the better part of a decade.

He was alright.

His grandson was still caught up in the life. I knew Grams could take care of herself, but the idea of her being connected to anyone I grew up around made me nervous.

"I've been up here a few years. I miss home sometimes, but this is home now too," Denise said.

"Ah, LA is gorgeous, especially in the fall. I'm sure you miss your family." Denise pasted on a fake smile and ran her hand through her hair.

Denise didn't like to talk about her family, but I couldn't blame her, neither did I. When she reached back, the sleeve of her shirt lifted and the marks on her skin were on full display.

Grams's eyes caught the bruises and her mouth thinned. She looked away and started to spin her water glass.

"And the weather, too," Denise threw in, trying to defuse the tension that was coming off Grams. She hadn't realized her sleeve had moved.

"Excuse me a minute. I'm going to run to the restroom," Grams turned to go up the stairs.

I looked at her, confused. There was a restroom right behind her.

Grams turned around and gave me a sad smile. I understood, she needed a minute.

"Sorry, I don't want to lay my baggage on your grandmother," Denise said, running her hand through her hair again.

"Don't apologize." I said, my fingers tightening on her thigh.

"This looks like an amazing place to grow up in," she said, looking at the house.

I nodded. "It was." I cleared my throat, "Grams does this thing, every two years on New Year's Eve. We pick a color together and we paint. This room has been every color under the sun."

Taking a fortifying breath, I continued. "When my mom passed, she let me choose black. But, she told me, complicated memories need an anchor. Something that reminds you of the joy before the hurt. My mama had this giant disco ball that she kept hanging in her room. I told Grams we were going to keep it black, but it was gonna sparkle. And we kept that sparkly black paint until we both decided we were ready for a change."

"An anchor," she repeated, her fingers caressing the tips of my fingers against her thigh. "I love the idea of that. A moment of joy for a moment of pain."

Pulling her chair toward me, I leaned in to kiss her, pouring everything I was feeling into her lips. I needed her to know she didn't have to feel alone anymore. That I would be here for her. That I was everything she needed. That she could choose me.

But for her to choose me, *really* choose me, she had to know all the things I was keeping buried. Honesty was necessary to keep her, but it was also the reason I was going to lose her.

CHAPTER 26
DENISE

Hugh was apparently a nickname. *Huey* spent the majority of his childhood here with his grandmother. It was the two of them against the world.

Huey played all the sports, because, *of course*, he was a jock in school.

"And what does that mean?" Hugh asked, raising his eyebrows.

"I mean, of course you *relished* being the center of attention," I replied, rolling my eyes.

"And what did you do?" His tone was playful.

"Advanced placement classes." I sniffed, throwing my nose in the air.

"Nerd."

"Dunce."

I stuck out my tongue at him and turned to see Grams smiling.

In between the history lesson, we ate, and we laughed. But did we eat!

Let me tell you, Grams could throw down. Macaroni and cheese, pot roast, green beans, fried green tomatoes, and fresh sourdough. I felt a brief pang for what life could've been like if I'd had a bigger family. That was a sad thought, and I didn't want to do sad thoughts today. Not here.

I pushed away the thoughts of my childhood and focused on the heat from Hugh's palm on my knee. We'd been there for hours, and the entire time he hadn't stopped touching me. And I loved it.

Feeling the warmth of his skin through my clothes grounded me. I didn't realize how nervous I'd been to meet her and to see this side of his life. But with him next to me, it all felt so easy.

"That potato salad was fantastic, I'm gonna need the recipe," Grams said, and with the way her eyes lit up, I knew she meant it.

"I'm happy to share it," I replied, smiling, glad that she'd enjoyed it.

Grams leaned back in her seat as her eyes bounced to Hugh and then me.

"So, how did this finally happen?" Grams cleared her throat. I could tell she'd wanted to ask all day.

"I gave her a glass of champagne." Technically, it was true. His hand squeezed my thigh.

Heat singed my cheeks and she laughed.

"I can see that wasn't all you gave her." Grams winked and Hugh groaned loudly before grabbing me and kissing my forehead.

"Grams, come on. Please, you promised you'd behave."

"Oh, she likes it." Grams pushed the empty water pitcher his way and shooed him out to refill it. She leaned forward to look around the corner towards the kitchen.

"He reminds me so much of his mama, it hurts." Pain laced her words, and I reached out for her hand. It couldn't have been easy for her to raise a child that looked like the one she'd lost.

"Huey was a little fucking tyrant for years, but he got his shit together. I was so relieved that I wasn't going to lose him too."

She smiled and looked back at me.

"And then he started working at Foxx... All he ever talked about was work and more work. Then suddenly it was, work is good, Denise did this, or 'Denny wore the shit out of this pink suit, you should've seen it'. I'm so glad he found you."

I stopped breathing. Me?

"Wow," I whispered.

"He's a good man. I can tell you're a good woman. You two deserve to find happiness with each other. Grab it while you can, Sugar. Let that anchor you and keep you from floating away. You never know where life will try and take you if you don't."

Before I could think too hard about her words, Hugh came in and plopped the water down.

"Just so you know, he was a terrible football player," she whispered.

I covered my mouth, looking up at him with a giggle.

Hugh shook his head.

"Okay, whatever this conspiratorial thing is between you two, it's gotta stop." He crossed his arms in front of him, his t-shirt flexing against his muscles.

I raised my eyebrows. *Ruh-roh.*

"Huey, you don't get to tell me to do a damn thing after I spent my prime hoe years wiping your ass and taking you to football practice."

I was leaning against Grams's chair, wheezing with laughter, while she stood and started wagging her finger in his face.

"I could've put it down on every single one of your coaches, but I didn't. And now you're trying to ruin what little fun I have left!"

The more she talked, the more Hugh looked like he was torn between mortification and wishing for a sudden and painless death. I, on the other hand, was saving this moment in my brain.

The mighty Huey, dressed down by his grandma in front of company.

CHAPTER 27
DENISE

Hugh stood there, stone-faced, as I wrote my potato salad recipe and laughed at some joke I told with his Grams. She was leaning on me like we'd known each other for ages. After she'd told him off, she gave him a kiss on the cheek and sat back down beside me, announcing she had an appointment so we'd only get to stay for a little bit longer.

Her shoulder hit my side and her eyes went wide. When she turned her back, I gave Hugh a wink and saw his nostrils flare.

"It was lovely to meet you," I said, lightheaded from hours of cackling at the top of my lungs.

"You better be coming by next week, Sugar. Hugh can come too, I guess. And maybe you can make that peach crumble."

"I am in!" I walked out the door first to give them a moment while I looked around the neighborhood.

It was dark and the street was quiet. It felt odd to be surrounded by homes that seemed to be dripping in history. Each of them had to be over a hundred years old.

I breathed deep, allowing the scent of redwoods to fill my lungs.

It smells like camping.

It was the thought that always popped into my head when I was out of the city.

A reminder that we used to do daddy/daughter camping trips when I was a kid. My dad was obsessed with me knowing how to rough it in the wild. And, by wild, he meant tents, sleeping bags, and pre-packed meals.

Before I could dismiss the memory, I stopped and thought back to what Hugh said about anchors. Happy memories that you could cling to in the face of the sad ones.

Camping was an anchor.

In spite of it all, it was the place where me and my father bonded under the stars.

Those moments with him didn't last forever. Eventually, he left and moved on.

Mom knew he'd never planned to stay, but she chose a few moments of happiness with him and built a family because she wanted to live at that moment for as long as she could.

I don't think she ever regretted it, but I never had the courage to ask her about it. I'd spent so long being angry.

At her and at him, but what if I chose to focus on the good? Would that help me see past my rage when I talked about them?

Hugh never talked about his mother either, but he did today. I saw the discomfort in his face, but the way he talked about his grief, the way they found a way to push through it together, it was beautiful.

Today was also a reminder that there was a lot we didn't know about each other. We had to change that. We needed to pry. Because if there was anything I'd learned, it was that I couldn't be with someone that I didn't communicate with.

Wait, were we... together?

CHAPTER 28
HUGH

I watched Grams squeeze Denise tight, tighter than I expected, before letting her go. Denise gave me a smile before giving a little nod from me to my Grams. She walked out the door and down the driveway to give us a little time to chat.

We stood together on the steps and when Denise had made it to the end of the driveway, Grams spoke.

"Huey," Grams grabbed my arm, her grip tight. "What aren't you telling me?"

I didn't have to ask. She wanted to know about the bruise.

Grams was my rock. I told her everything. I knew I'd have to fess up to what happened on Friday when I came today, but it was still hard to utter the words out loud. I swore I'd never break her heart again.

"Grams, I handled it." She looked in my eyes before placing her hand over my heart.

"And what does that mean?" The question was soft.

"Grammy, you didn't see her. See her place. I had to."
My hand reached out to her shoulder, and she just looked
at me, like she was trying to piece together a puzzle. After
a moment, she nodded.

"Love pushes and it pulls."

"*Love*? Grams, please." I shook my head and blew out
a breath.

"You've been talking about this girl for years. Yes, *love*,
you silly damn fool." Her hand came out to box my ear
and I dodged it.

"She does more than push and pull," I said, sneaking a
peek at her. She had her head lifted to the sky, the soft skin
of her neck extending out from beneath her jacket. I
didn't realize I was absently following the trail of my
tattoo until Grams' eyes caught on to the movement.
Reaching for me, she placed her hand over mine.

"You're here. You. Not him." Her words stole my
breath.

"Grams, I—"

"Are you in jail? Did you have to bury that man's
body?"

"I stopped—"

Her hand went back to my chest.

"If you were still him, you wouldn't have stopped."

Reaching up, she grabbed my face with both of her
hands, so I wouldn't have a choice but to look in her eyes.

"When I say love pushes and pulls, I mean, we sometimes do things for love that scare us."

She gave my face a shake.

"If you hadn't been him, you wouldn't be you, and where would you be?"

She let the weight of her words lie for a minute before she pinched my cheeks.

"I'm not saying that God tests us, because I know how that makes you feel. But, I will say, you are where you're supposed to be. And so is she. Don't fear that."

She was right. I was afraid. I trusted Denise. I *knew* Denise. It was time that Denise knew me, too.

"I have to tell her," I said more to myself than Grams.

"Yes, you do," she agreed.

She dragged me down the stairs and I watched my feet hit one step and then another.

"I don't want to fuck this up," I whispered.

Grams pulled me into her arms and squeezed me tight, twisting and turning me like she always did.

"It's just a little push, baby, if she's the right one, she'll pull," she said into my ear. "But, she ain't as fragile as you think."

I laughed as she let me go. She was right about that. If there's anything I'd learned in the last forty-eight hours, it's that.

I started to back away, smiling and feeling lighter than I had in days.

"I hope so, Grams."

"Have a little faith. She's gonna pick this year's color. Mark my words."

The image of Denise with me and Grams looking over paint samples made me dizzy. And *love*? Did I love Denise? Of course. I loved my friend, Denise. But, did I *love* Denise?

I looked at her, standing in the semi-darkness. Then I saw her prancing around SFMOMA, watched her drunken smile as we sat in her new office and stared at the city below us, saw her twirling around in the metallic dress as she made her way through a room full of some of the most intimidating people in our world like she'd grown up surrounded by billions of dollars.

My hand rubbed at a sudden feeling in my chest. Grams was the most perceptive woman I'd ever met. As I looked at this stunning woman, I wondered if that fluttery ache that happened only when she was near was what love feels like.

CHAPTER 29
DENISE

My mind was still contemplating what exactly it was that I was doing with Hugh when his hand slid into mine. Our ride pulled in front of the driveway and I looked back at Grams as she waved, blowing us a kiss from her spot on the stairs.

I waved back as Hugh whispered in my ear, "She absolutely adores you."

"Good, I definitely like her more than you."

I looked up at him and he pressed his lips to mine, stealing the air from my lungs.

When I gasped in surprise, he took advantage. Slipping his tongue against mine, rough and insistent, I felt my body melt into his. Whatever this was between us was foreign to me. He was taking as much as he was giving, he filled my cup more than I poured mine out. The control I had on everything in my life was slipping away, but for the first time I wasn't scared of loosening my hold.

This man.

I sighed into his mouth. His thumb flexed against my throat, and I knew he wanted to squeeze it tight. He was getting lost in me as much as I was already lost in him.

Hugh pulled away reluctantly. Before he could get too far, I grabbed his shirt to bring him back to my mouth for one more taste. I licked at the seam of his mouth before I bit down on his lip. My tease earned me a groan. I smiled, pulling back and biting my own lip.

"You know Hugh has a whole condo you can break in." Grams yelled out from the porch.

I tried to push Hugh away, my cheeks hot and my core heavy, but he grabbed me and pulled me tight to his side.

"Goodbye, Grams. We'll see you next weekend," he called out, clearly not feeling any shame in kissing me like that in front of God and everybody.

Grams laughed, long and loud as she replied, "I'll see you next week, babies."

He held open the car door and reached out to palm my ass while I slid into the back of the sedan. Smacking his hand, I felt heat rising in my cheeks. The driver didn't say a word and I thanked the heavens for that small miracle.

After he slid in through his own door, his palm connected back with mine and I looked down at it. As the city flashed by, I thought of seeing Grams again and the thought made me feel gooey inside.

Belly full and laughed out, I leaned my head against Hugh's shoulder and watched the city drift by.

"I'm going to get ready for the morning," I said.

We'd just gotten back, and it was starting to get late.

It was the last thing that I wanted to do. Going through my clothes was going to be a rabbit hole. I spent so much money and time building my wardrobe. I hadn't even managed to grab half of it. Looking at what I had was going to confirm all that I'd lost. I sighed, trying to prepare myself as I walked into the spare bedroom.

Hugh followed behind me. When I grabbed the first case, he watched as I unzipped it. Something passed across his face before he stepped inside, crossing over to the other side of me. Unzipping the other case, he grabbed a pair of shoes, walked over to the massive walk-in, and placed them on a shelf.

When I raised an eyebrow at him, he didn't say a word, just grabbed another pair of shoes and headed back to the closet.

"I wasn't going to—"

"We should talk," Hugh said as he moved.

The bubble we'd built over the last few days was bound to pop, but I didn't realize it would have to be right now.

But it made sense. We had to work tomorrow, and we'd likely spend all of our time together in the coming weeks. I thought I would have to be the one to bring it all up, but Hugh was beating me to it.

I nodded and tried to hide the immediate nervousness that zipped through me.

"We should," I agreed.

I grabbed a dress and hugged it close, using it like a shield to hide the unease clawing around in my stomach.

He was holding a pair of pumps in his hands, "I know our agreement is done." He turned to face me. "You can obviously stay here for as long as you need—"

I blinked at him, adjusting the hanger in the dress.

"Wait, I'm confused."

"We made the agreement for a reason." Hugh looked at the suitcase before grabbing the bag and tipping it over, moving to sort its contents.

"We did," I replied.

"I want to move at your pace. I'm ready to talk whenever you are."

"Okay," I said.

"Good," he replied, matching up pairs of shoes and setting aside wrinkled slacks.

"No, I mean, okay. I'm ready now." I clarified.

He looked up from his neat piles and gave me an incredulous look.

"I didn't mean now. And I should probably—"

"We work together." I cut him off. I needed to say the words I'd been rehearsing in my head for the last hour. "I wanted to avoid making a mess of what we had. And yeah, it's gotten messy, but it's a good mess."

I reached out to grab his hand. He cleared his throat while his hand tightened on mine.

"Stop." Hugh's tone was sad, almost vulnerable.

I opened and closed my mouth. Hugh leaned closer to me and took a steeling breath.

"Before you keep going, I need to tell you the truth. About Switch."

CHAPTER 30
HUGH

Grabbing her hand, I pulled Denise to sit down on the bed. She was confused. As much as it hurt me, I let go of her hand and scooted back to give her some space. I'd never done this before, the whole naked honesty thing, but I knew she deserved to know before she made any decision about her path forward.

"You asked me about my tattoo, and I said that it was Switch."

Denise nodded, confused and unsure of where I was going with this.

"I was angry when my mom passed. I blamed everyone for her being gone. Grams tried to take me to church, she took me to psychologists, but none of that helped. There was this darkness in me that no light could touch. Only darkness could and I let it in."

She was silent.

I didn't expect her to understand. Darkness summoned darkness. There was never any real temptation for me before that. The second that angry pit filled my soul, it was a siren call to those around me drowning in their own fury.

"I fell in with some bad people."

Wasn't that always the story? One misstep, one glance and suddenly I was in a crew, and they were my new family. They knew and accepted my rage, while also using it to their advantage.

"I hurt people. For them, for us, and because it felt good."

I was looking past Denise, now. I couldn't bear to see her reaction. I would lose my nerve. And I needed to get through this. To say the words and show her the real me. The one that sat behind a door that was cracked and oozing drips of inky black that blended with the vibrant green that she'd slipped in without me realizing it.

"Switch—Switchblade—was sneaky and stayed in the shadows. No one expected a kid to come for them. I carved people, maimed people. Most of them were guilty, but a few weren't."

That was the part that hurt the most to remember. Hurting bad people, that was easier for me to accept, to comprehend, because they were a part of that life. But the people that just got caught up, the fear in their eyes, was something that still haunted me.

"I didn't have some grand epiphany, not really. It was just a dream. We'd painted over the sparkly black wall that day, and that night I saw my mom. I was at some kind of ceremony, and she had on a sparkly black dress, and she was screaming and jumping up and down. I woke up feeling warm for the first time in a long time."

Denise's hands covered mine, but I couldn't look at her.

"So, I told them I was out. And they said they would let me, I just had to do something that would cement me to them forever, in case I ever flipped."

I could feel Denise's fingers tightening on mine, but I couldn't see her, I could only see him.

The alley was dark, but the cherry of his cigarette flaming gave me a hint of his shadowy face. My hands were sweaty as I walked over to him. I wasn't dumb, I played up my age, I even had an empty backpack slung over my shoulder.

Gripping the switchblade tight in my pocket, I looked up at him and paused.

"Rudy?"

He looked at me, still puffing on the cigarette between his lips.

"Why?"

I gave him an innocent smile, even though I could feel the sweat beading at my neck beneath my hoodie.

"My moms sent me, she said to give you the money she owes."

He leaned closer and he smiled.

"And who's your m—"

He didn't get out the word. I'd dug the blade into his neck and pulled as hard as I could to the side before I ran. I ran and I ran. I didn't stop until I saw an encampment. They had a few buckets on fire, and I knew I was covered in evidence.

"Do you mind?" I asked, my voice shaking.

The black man was older, and he watched me warily before shaking his head.

I stripped down—taking off my jeans, my sweater, my shirt, my shoes—and wiped furiously at the blood on my skin before throwing it all into the flames.

Standing there in my tank top and bs, the burning smell of nylon rose up and stung my nose. I was still holding the knife. I didn't know what to do with it. It wouldn't turn to ash if I burned it, and I couldn't keep it.

After a moment, a hand reached out and grabbed the knife. I watched that man pull the pieces apart, wipe it clean, and throw a few pieces into the fire and the rest into his basket.

"I better not see you again," his voice was angry, but his tone was soft. His hand wiped at tears on my cheek. I hadn't even realized I was crying.

"Fix your face and go on home."

And I did.

"I killed him. It wasn't on the news or anything, but I heard that they'd found a body. But I was out, so I didn't ask questions. It was a long time ago, but it's something that I carry with me, someone that I put away."

I stood, not being able to handle sitting anymore.

"The tattoo is a reminder of what I did for my second chance. But Switch is still in here, I can't pretend he's not. You deserved the truth. I'm sorry, I'll just leave you here to pack or unpack."

I walked away, fighting every urge to look back at her. She hadn't said anything. I didn't even know what I would say if someone hit me with something like that it.

Saying those words and reliving those moments, that had been much harder than I expected it to be. I hadn't thought about that man in decades. I'd refused to. He was a bad man. One of the guys in my crew, Ricky, had said he'd roughed up some girl he knew. He was guilty. That's probably why the cops didn't look too hard into his murder.

They'd never found me.

I didn't know what was going to happen next. If I'd wake up and find Denise gone. If I had just ruined everything. But I had to do it. I had to tell her. I'd spent a long time being disciplined and rigid, but like Grams said, I needed to take a chance and push.

I needed to be honest because that's what Denise deserved.

And Denise deserved me, even if I didn't deserve her.

CHAPTER 31
DENISE

Hugh left before I got up the next morning. I hadn't gotten much sleep, and I was sure he hadn't either. At two, I heard soft clinking come from the kitchen, but I stayed in the guest room, still trying to process what he'd told me.

He was a killer?

No, Switch was a killer.

He wasn't Switch anymore. He wasn't even Huey anymore. He was Hugh.

I sat there, silent, taking it all in and trying to reconcile this man with the version of himself he was talking about. The shame that laced the features of his handsome face as he talked, the way he became lost in his memories, refusing to look at me.

The kid he was talking about wasn't anything like the man sitting in front of me. Remorse made his hands shake. I reached out to grab him, but I don't think he even remembered I was there. He looked like he was moving underwater, his words slow and measured.

Then he left.

A part of me felt thankful for it. I didn't know what to say to him at the time. I was unsure what to expect when he started his story, but I know how it made me feel: sad.

I thought back to when I was twelve. My dad had just left and I was furious. With him, with my mom, but mostly with myself. Because I didn't want to care. I'd somehow convinced myself that caring made me vulnerable, left things out of my control.

But, I was never not a rule follower. A nerd. I paid my taxes. I'd never gotten in trouble with anyone before, but I'd seen it. Kids around me carrying shit for adults, dealing drugs at school. I avoided it all because I was lasered-focused on graduating, so I could leave and never come back.

But what would've happened if things had gone differently for me? If I'd been pulled into something that I had only one way out of?

I thought of Hugh having to make that choice and I understood him, why he became the man he did. He owed it to himself to be the best version of himself that he could be. He sacrificed something in himself for a second chance.

I spent the night thinking about it. Trying to figure out what this all meant in the context of the man I'd known for years.

But, I couldn't see anything. There were no threads that connected the two that I'd ever seen. I was realizing I'd never even heard Hugh raise his voice. In almost three years, even when work was stressful, when someone's pipes above him burst, when his car got stolen from a client meeting, he never yelled.

He respected my boundaries. When I didn't want to talk about what happened, he gave me space, he didn't insist on me talking to him. He asked if I was okay. His grounding presence wasn't volatile, it was caring. That, that was the Hugh I knew.

I heard my dad's voice in my head, "Necessity is the mother of invention."

It was something my dad used to say. I think it was some proverb but, knowing him, it was something he heard in some 80s action flick.

Someone saw a child, confused and in pain, and turned that kid into a weapon.

I was sad for Huey. Sad that his grief was twisted and mangled, and that Grams had to watch him descend into it.

But, that was before I knew him. The Hugh that I know came out the other side a better man. And yeah, his shit was dark, darker than mine, but he was still Hugh. I'd spent the afternoon thinking about how we needed to get to know each other, to really see past the surface to see if whatever it was that was between us was real. And Hugh gave that to me.

That wasn't going to scare me away.

CHAPTER 32
DENISE

It was a ten-minute walk to the office from Hugh's condo. My suitcases were still sitting on the ground, full of clothes, so I grabbed the only thing I'd managed to hang the night before. I opted against trying to find his iron and hung the dress next to the shower to steam and hopefully de-wrinkle.

I opted for a pair of thigh high boots to go with my vivid dress. I said a small prayer of thanks that my boots had survived, I'd spent hundreds of dollars on them, and they'd been on sale.

The dress had an empire waist snatched right below my breasts and flared out to a full, unlined skirt. So full that if I twirled, it would flare out all the way. It was one of my favorite features on a dress, but that's not what made me pay the exorbitant price tag. It was the colors.

The dress was like a watercolor painting, each color flaring bright and fighting for dominance. When I saw it, I saw myself. It felt like the perfect dress for the day. My arm was much less sore, but I knew I had to hide it, so I chose a pink blazer to go over the top and threw on my camel trench coat to keep me warm for the walk.

When I made it into the office, I gave Bill a wave, adjusting my briefcase on my shoulder.

"Hey there," I said, giving him a smile.

"Denise! Good morning," he said.

I nodded, pressing my palm against the scanner and heading up.

A few people were already in the office. I gave tiny waves as I made my way to my desk and threw everything on top before heading over to Hugh's office.

I knew what I was going to say when I got in. I'd been thinking about it for hours. All the right ways to frame it, to explain my thought processes and how I got to my conclusion. When I walked into his office, I shut the door behind me.

Hugh looked impeccable in his black shirt and... I knew that tie. It was one of the ones he'd used to tie me down that night. The gold sang against the black and it felt perfect for him. He looked up from his computer and took a deep breath.

Before I could stop myself, I walked over and plopped right on the edge of the desk to look at him.

"That's *your* tell."

He slowly looked from the desk to me before he spoke.

"My tell?" he said, looking distracted.

"When you're nervous or you feel uncomfortable, you take a deep breath, like you're looking to gain strength from that little bit of extra oxygen."

He didn't say anything, just stared.

"You left before me," I whispered, surprised that I sounded hurt. And I guess I had been, which seems silly in retrospect. It's not like I didn't know where to find him.

"I figured you needed space." He still wasn't looking at me. So, when I threw my carefully thought out plan out the window, he wasn't expecting it.

Grabbing the edge of his chair, I pulled him forward. I swung my legs around, straddled his hips and kissed him.

I swallowed his sound of surprise and swept my tongue past his lips, tasting the espresso on his tongue, inhaling his scent as he shook off his surprise as he grabbed my waist and pulled me closer, meeting every twist and turn of my tongue, matching the beat of what I was building between us.

I wanted him to feel what I felt when he kissed me, engulfed me, surrounded me in warmth and made me feel his affection. My body always awoke when Hugh was near, but I didn't explore his body, I focused on tightening my hands around his neck and feeling his pulse start to race, just like mine.

When I broke the kiss, we were both breathing hard, desperate for oxygen.

"Denise, you need to—"

"Shut up. You already talked. Now, I get to talk." I spoke the words against his mouth, my lips faintly caressing his.

"Was Curtis able to walk away? Stand up and leave that apartment?" I knew the answer to the question, but I needed him to hear himself say it.

Hugh nodded.

"Use your words." I demanded.

I felt his hands flex against my thighs.

"Yes," he replied.

"You are Hugh. Not Switch, not Huey. Hugh." I was looking right at him, I needed him to see that I saw, that I understood.

"This weekend was amazing. I want more like it."

He sucked in a breath, and I continued on.

"I have questions. Gaps that need to be filled. But, I'm not holding your past against you."

Hugh's head came to my chest and I held him tight to me.

We sat like this for a while, Hugh's fingers moving across the skin at the hem of my dress, me tracing the skin of his neck beneath his shirt collar.

"Thank you," he said, his lips moving against my skin.

He looked up at me, his eyes shining. I leaned down and brought my lips to his again, a chaste kiss that said more than words could at that moment.

"Now, I'm going to get up and we're going to take a look at the financials for the eight organizations that I picked from that list. A few of them are abroad. We can go through theirs first and try to get questions out to them before morning. If we're lucky, we'll get some replies before we head home tonight."

"Home?" He raised his eyebrows.

I hit his chest and started to stand. "You know what I mean. Don't start."

"And what if I want to start." His hands gripped my ass through the fabric of my skirt, and I tutted at him.

"I think it would be a bad look to get HR called on us at seven thirty on a Monday morning," I replied, taking a step back. "Plus, imagine telling your Grams we're unemployed because you wanted to start. I definitely don't want to get on that woman's bad side." I faked a shudder, but Hugh didn't laugh.

I looked over at him and pulled tight on his beard.

"Open your email. We have shit to do," I said, grabbing a chair and dragging it around the desk.

CHAPTER 33
HUGH

It was well past 8 p.m. as Denise and I sat, surrounded by piles of papers, at the big conference table in the office. We'd narrowed our list of eight down by two by comparing industry statistics and doing some digging online. The CFO one guy appointed had a recent felony. They were out. The numbers for a sustainable electronics company seemed bogus, so they were out too.

Falling into work was good, it was preferable. After the conversation we'd had this morning, I felt lighter than I'd felt in a long time.

Denise was the closest person to me, other than Grams. I had a few friends from college, but we talked once a year when they sent me their Christmas cards.

Knowing that Denise knew all the black edges of me and still sat here, laughing and joking over pasta, was hard to fathom. I'd never considered it. There was still things dancing between us and our relationship, but I had something I hadn't allowed myself to feel: hope.

Hope that she'd see me through the inky black and that she really want a relationship with me.

I watched as she chewed on a meatball and tapped the paper in front of her.

"Automation is the direction to go in. We can get that guy that Xavier knows, I can't remember his name, but he loves throwing money at anything that leverages AI. VacYay uses AI, real time weather updates, client satisfaction, ease of access, and satellite data to plan and adjust vacations. They even collaborate with locals to improve traveler safety. They're based out of Africa. And..."

She shuffles through another stack, taking another bite of pasta while I tapped VacYay into a search engine.

"They are already seeing a four thousand percent return on their investment. It looks like they crowdfunded."

I turned my laptop and showed her comments on their crowdfund page, lots of the investors went on discounted vacations and a cursory glance showed nothing negative.

"I feel comfortable considering them for the top three. But we'd need to fly out to see their operation," I said.

Denise rolled her eyes. "A forced trip to Nairobi? Twist my arm..."

I shook my head as she set VacYay away from the rest and started looking at another stack.

"Lucian will need some convincing, but what do you think about health tech?" I said, flipping over the page on the pile I was looking at.

"I mean, Theranos is still super fresh. I don't think he'd go for it."

"Maybe he feels like enough time has passed," I say, thinking out loud. "Would he have left them on the list if he wasn't interested in seeing what was out there?"

"Or, he left them in to see if we'd be dumb enough to consider one after he'd spent years calling Elizabeth Holmes an actual psychopath." Denise took a sip of her water and shrugged.

Lucian popped his head out of his office and glanced around until he saw us.

"Hey."

Denise squawked and turned around. We'd thought we were the only ones in the building this late.

"Does one of you know a Cleo?"

"I do," Denise said, standing, wiping at her mouth.

"I got a call from the front desk that some crazy person named Cleo was downstairs and wouldn't leave."

"What?" Denise and I said at the same time.

I tapped my pocket and realized my phone was at my desk. Oops.

Lucian walked over and opened the door just as Cleo was leaning forward to knock. She lost her balance and the two collided. Cleo swore, falling on top of him.

"Jesus, you're crushing my—"

"Hey, fuck you, man. I'm fine, thanks for asking, you douchebag."

Shit.

Denise ran over as Cleo clambered to her feet and glared down at Lucian, whose mouth was practically on the floor. Oh. I knew that look. That was going to be *interesting* to watch.

"Denise, you really gotta be better about your fucking phone. Hey, Fudge Pop."

"Cleo, what's wrong?" Denise asked.

Cleo was grabbing my computer and typing.

"I've been calling and texting both of you. Fucking workaholics," Cleo was huffing, clearly upset.

"Cleo," I said.

"Hey, don't Cleo, her with that voice." Denise raised an eyebrow, and I rolled my eyes.

"Denny, don't start," I replied.

"You both need to sit down. Wait, before you sit down, maybe you should grab a drink. Wait wait wait, no—"

"Someone needs to make fucking sense!" Lucian shouted.

The room went quiet, and all eyes moved back to Cleo.

Denise took a breath before saying, "Cleo, if you don't spit it the fuck out—"

"He was recording. It makes sense, he was streaming, we came in and then—"

"Who was recording what?" Lucian asked.

Cleo ignored Lucian and looked right at Denise.

"Curtis was streaming some fucking game. Then *you* came in. Then *I* came in. Babe, we're kind of all over the internet."

"WHAT!?" Denise screeched.

Cleo turned the computer. The title of the video was "Lying dude manhandles his fat girlfriend and gets his ass beat".

I clenched my teeth as she pressed play. We watched as Denise talked at Curtis, watched as he screamed in Denise's face before all hell broke loose. Curtis hobbled over and shut the camera off, his face wet.

"Where is this asshole," Lucian asked.

I hadn't heard him get closer to me, but I shook my head.

"Gone, I handled it, but it looks like these ladies didn't really need me," I said, wishing I'd done a whole lot more than make that fucking prick piss himself.

"You sure?" All eyes turned to Lucian. He was furious.

"He's not worth it, man." I said, my tone measured.

"That was a nice tackle," Lucian said, looking at Cleo.

"Eat me," she replied.

I stifled my laugh.

"Your mom called me, Denise. Someone sent it to her."

Denise was still staring at the video. I don't even think she'd heard us. I touched her shoulder and she startled.

"I'd really like off the merry-go-round," she said.

I threaded my fingers with hers and closed the computer. Not before seeing that it had been up two days and already hit a million views.

Fuck.

"What do we do now?" she asked.

That was a good fucking question.

Hugh and Denise will return one final(ish) time.

ABOUT THE AUTHOR

Thank you for diving into Ayla Cox's world for a little while.

When Ayla's not on her knees in a fit of passion and lust, she's devouring any book she can get her hands on.

On the off chance that Ayla has time off, you may find her frolicking on a beach or hiding away in a lake cabin, recharging her batteries, both figuratively and literally.

If you love what you've read, give her a follow and leave a few encouraging words.

Ayla Cox can be found on TikTok @AylaCoxWrites and on Instagram @AylaCoxWrites.

FROM AYLA'S DESK

Umm. Hi! Wow. Thank you so much for reading and loving the Just a Taste series! I wouldn't have gotten this together without the love and support that I get every day from readers like you. I want to send a special shout out to the folks that know Ayla in real life and have been my support this last year.

2023 was both invigorating and terrifying, but all of that was worth it because it brought me here. To a place where I finally did the thing that used to scare me the most: publishing my writing.

I want to take a minute to give a special thank you to my team:

Brianna Mbog, thank you for being a glorious assistant! You see me and you breathe so much positivity into me and I wouldn't be here without it. Thank you for being my alpha reader and for being my sounding board when my brain is just not working haha.

Eline F. Roman, thank you for helping bring Denise and Hugh to life! You are immensely talented, and you truly bring so much joy and care to your work. I can't imagine anyone else I would trust with bringing my words to life.

Lastly, I just want to thank you, dear reader. I started writing a long time ago because I felt like I couldn't see women that looked like me in fiction. I know some of you may feel that way too. It's important to me that the worlds that I create bridge that gap. I hope you found something here that made you feel seen because I see you. The world sees you. And I think you're magnificent.

STILL HERE?

You'll see Hugh and Denise again, I promise!